Werewolf Hunter

Tobias Halson: Book 2

John Evans

Cover Art Design by: Kelly Moran/Rowan Prose Publishing
Photo Credit: Adobe Images/Deposit Photos
First Edition
ISBN: 978-1-961967-57-1
Rowan Prose Publishing, LLC
www.RowanProsePublishing.com
Published in the United States of America

Other works by John Evans:

"That dog is neither man nor monster. Only a man can truly hope to kill a monster."
~Alucard, Hellsing

Chapter 1

Don't get me wrong, I don't hate kids, and I think when it comes to educating our youth, first-hand experience is the best teacher. I'm a firm believer in Tolkien's old adage "the burned hand teaches best," and kids these days are too damn coddled. We would have so much fewer spoiled brats if more kids had to graduate from the school of hard knocks. Sadly, the Order had a different idea of "first-hand experience" when it came to teaching newbie hunters about the trade.

My first time had been more than a lesson in hard knocks. I had nearly died and was terrified the whole time. My first hunt had ended with a broken arm, jaw, and nose, plus countless bruises and cuts that hurt for weeks. I had wildly overestimated my abilities and underestimated my prey. That's what kids do. They believe they are invincible until the world bites them on the ass and sobers them up. I'd been fourteen at the time, and accidentally stumbled into a vampire nest.

Oh yeah, did I mention I'm a vampire hunter? Because that's kind of important. I'm not making it up. I really am a totally badass vampire hunter. I have a license and everything. Okay, my license is actually for pest extermination and animal control, but I do have an official title and decree from the Order and all that. I even have a crossbow. I've never used it, but I have one.

The Order is exactly what it sounds like, a group of doddery old men, most of them Oxford-educated with British accents, sitting around with mountains of old leather-bound books, all of whom have been hunting the creatures of the night since before I was an itch in my father's underwear. Though I doubt any of them had so much as seen a vampire in the last twenty or thirty years. Getting a top spot in the Order was a cushiony job for the geezers to sit around telling old war stories and ordering the younger generations around.

It had been a hell of a learning experience, my first hunt. I'd peed my pants and fled in terror, lucky to have survived. I'd been much more careful from then on until I learned to be cleverer than the undead monsters I hunted.

Flurries of snow drifted from the coal-black night sky. Only a couple of days 'til Christmas, and the temperature had been steadily dropping. The weather people were calling for lower temperatures and storm fronts bringing more snow. It was starting to look like the city of Philadelphia was going to have a white Christmas. The cold made my old injuries throb, especially the scar along my back where a vampire had nearly torn my spine out when I was nine.

So, why was I, the greatest vampire hunter who ever lived, wasting my time teaching kids on a cold, dark night in the middle of winter? Well, turns out, those big paychecks and extravagant perks come with a price. There are no paychecks, and the only perks are people thinking you're crazy, so you can see why I was less than enthusiastic about bringing some snot-nosed brats up to speed. The Order had charged me with helping these brats get their first kill and show them how it was to be done.

These two kids could not have been greener. I mean it. They were literally turning green out of fear and horror. Jake, the boy, looked like he was about to toss his cookies and run home crying to Mommy. He was nineteen and a little over six feet tall. He was well built, not muscular, but not gangly. More along the lines of a swimmer or runner. His face still had traces of acne on his cheeks and forehead, just below his sandy blond hair. I could see that, given a few years and some experience, he would be the poster boy for the Order's vampire hunters.

Cassie was a stark contrast. While she was only a few inches shorter than Jake, she seemed a little more held together, though she still managed to look pale with her Black complexion. She had big brown eyes that made her resemble one of those American Girls dolls, innocent and so out of place in such a violent calling. The Order didn't discriminate when it came to gender, but deep down, I had an urge to protect her from what she was seeing. Call me a misogynist, but a girl her age should've been out hanging with friends and goofing off at the mall. She should be more concerned with homework and worrying about getting into a good college. Not standing in the middle of an empty industrial complex parking lot, freezing her butt off, about to watch something so horrifying, it would give her nightmares for the rest of her life.

Both kids were staring at an improvised dais made of concrete blocks, rebar, and what looked like an entire hardware store's worth of chains. All of this was necessary to keep the screaming and thrashing vampire restrained. She'd been one of those little goth kids. You know, the ones who wore black torn clothing and dog collars, who dyed their hair black, plastering on lipstick and eyeliner. The black only made her pale skin appear to glow like ghost light. I guess she would've been pretty, if you're into emo chicks, except for the dagger-like fangs she snapped at me as I walked in a circle around the makeshift platform.

Both of the teenagers stood well back, away from the tied-up vampire. Their fear made them appear years younger than they were. Each of them held a large wooden stake and a mallet, in addition to wearing large, bulky wooden crosses around their necks. They looked ridiculous. The way they were standing and holding their tools in front of them were like actors in a play getting ready to go on stage. While there was still some danger from the vampire, this was as safe as it was going to get for them, and they were frozen in place.

"Okay, kids, listen up." I addressed them in a loud voice as I passed behind them. "This is your final test before the Order green lights you for your first hunt. It doesn't get easier than this because the next time you see a vampire, it will probably be trying to kill you."

Jake's Adam's apple jumped up and down in his throat, and Cassie broke out in nervous flop sweat.

I paused behind them so all they could see was themselves and the monster in front of them.

"So," I continued. "Who can tell me what we have here?"

"A-a v-vampire," Cassie stammered as the vampire gave a particularly hard lurch, and the chains rattled and strained.

They both flinched at the sudden movement.

"Yes. What kind of vampire?" I asked.

"Just a regular vampire, I think," Jake answered.

I smacked him in the back of the head.

"Look at her!" I barked. "What can you tell me about her?" It came out harsher than I'd meant it to, but I was cold. They needed to unlearn some of the crap the Order teaches as doctrine and see beyond the simple and limited views of textbook knowledge.

They jumped at my voice, as they had in reaction to the vampire trying to break free. Fear is a powerful motivator. While it can cause you to freeze up, once you master it, you can use it to your advantage. The sooner they embraced fear, the better, because they'd be experiencing a lot of it.

"She's a young girl, late teens," Jake stated, trying to recover from his earlier error.

"Like most young impressionable youths, she's part of an alternative culture that commonly worships darkness and has a perceived view of creatures of the night like vampires, mostly in part to modern re-imagining and glorification of these beings. Thus, they are easy prey for vampires and can be dangerous zealous followers, even when not under a vampire's influence, as they refuse to believe in the true nature of the monsters." Cassie rattled off a near-textbook and fairly apt description of the typical kid our vampire had been.

I wondered where she'd picked that up. I doubted the scholars of the Order had managed to update their doctrine.

For the longest time, even up until I'd first begun training to hunt vampires, their modus operandi had been very paleolithic. Ugh, find vampire. Ugh, stake vampire. Ugh, brag. Ugh, ugh. It was nice to see that the times might be changing for the better. Younger hunters like myself had been campaigning for the Order to better educate the new candidates more about the people who were potential vampire prey, so they better understand the psychology behind modern vampires. Sort of a "know thy enemy" Tsun Su vibe, but getting the older Order members to change something decades old was nearly impossible.

"Right." I'd admit, she impressed me. "These days, modern sub and alternative cultures, especially the gothic and dark stuff, are extremely susceptible to vampires. Thanks to over fifty years of bad movies and television, people have forgotten what vampires are. And what *are* vampires?"

"Monsters." They both chorused as if they were school kids answering in unison.

"Right, kids." I walked around them and ran my hand through my long, dark hair. "I've been instructed to teach you guys how to kill a vampire properly. Now, since I have only one, you are gonna have to share, and I'm only going to teach you how to manually ensure that a vampire is dead and stays dead. So, we will have to skip the sunlight demonstration."

The vampire turned her face towards me and snapped her jaws so viciously, she actually made an audible clack when her teeth clicked together.

"Now, first, let's go through the basic tools." I pulled out a black duffle bag that was heavy with gear. "Other than sunlight, what else hurts a vampire?"

"Crosses," Jake answered, glancing quickly down at his own cross.

"Yes and no," I addressed him directly. "Crosses only work if you're a believer in the Christian faith. Holy items, also known as items of faith, work on your own unwavering belief in that symbol. So, if you don't believe in the symbol, then it can't protect you. Or, if you don't believe strongly enough, it might not be strong enough to shield you from a vampire. So, any symbol of any faith will work, be it the Bible, the Quran, heck even Ronald Reagan will channel your faith into a warding shield against a vampire."

"Don't you believe in God?" Cassie asked. She had obviously noticed my lack of a holy item.

"I don't believe in cruel gods," I replied in a rather matter-of-fact manner.

She recoiled as if I'd insulted her faith.

Give her a few years. She would either become a blind follower of religion in order to deal with the terror of the darkness or she would learn the truth like I had—that there is no God, only endless darkness full of evil.

"What else?" I asked, trying to move things along. Dawn was only a few hours away.

"Holy water?" This time from Jake, who seemed unsure of his answer and scared of another admonishment from me.

"Correct," I said to Jake's apparent surprise. "And what makes holy water different from other holy items?" Both looked at me nonplussed, and I sighed. "Holy items work on *your* faith." I put emphasis on the "your" part. "Holy water is an exception, as it works on *another* person's faith." I stressed the word as I had previously. "Generally, the priest or whoever blessed it."

As I talked, I pulled out a plastic sports bottle with a squeeze top. I held it up so they could see it. I popped the top and then pointed it at the vampire's face. Giving it a squeeze, a jet of water shot out and hit the creature in the face like a squirt gun.

The vampire roared and screamed. She tossed her head. Her punk-styled hair flipped from side to side, but you could clearly see the effect the blessed water had on her flesh. Her skin roiled and broke out into sores and blisters as if the bottle had been full of acid instead of just water. The boils then burst open and oozed yellowish-green puss. The smell was strong and horrible, causing all three of us to cover our noses and mouths.

I will give them credit. Neither of them threw up as I had my first time.

The vamp's skin began to heal and clear up, the flesh knitting itself back together as we watched, and her pain subsided. Within minutes, she looked as if nothing had ever happened. Both of my students were staring in slack-jawed awe at the healing power. It's actually quite impressive when you see it for the first time. It's a lot like a magic trick. You know what you saw, but it can't be real. Once you accept that it is and have witnessed it a few times, it becomes boring and, in the wrong situations, annoying. Vampires can heal nearly any wound given enough time, even being beheaded.

"Moving on," I called to them, trying to speed things along. "What else?"

They stood there, staring at me. I could tell their minds were racing to try and figure out what was next and to recover from what they'd just seen.

"Garlic?" volunteered Jake, seemingly excited by the prospect of another demonstration.

"No. Garlic doesn't work."

His face fell a little.

"Now, the garlic myth is actually based on the vampire's hyper-acute senses. They have noses better than most blood-hounds. However, this can be exploited by overloading these senses. Smelly foods like garlic can overwhelm younger vampires who don't have control of their new powers. I once heard of a hunter who knocked out a vampire with a bad bean burrito he had for lunch."

This set both of them giggling. I wasn't sure how much truth there was to the story, but it even brought a smile to my face.

"I can smell you haven't bathed in years," said a voice from just below me.

Oh, great. The first time the vampire speaks, and she insults me. Young people these days, I tell you.

"Oi! Shut it." I smacked the vampire on her forehead.

She snarled and returned to wailing and thrashing.

"What about guns?"

I looked up at Jake, who'd asked the question. When I'd moved to hit the vamp, my long duster coat had swung open, and they had no doubt seen the old Colt 1911 I carried in a shoulder holster under the coat. I gave them both a sly smile as I reached into the dark folds of my coat and drew out the big .45.

I held it up so they could both see it clearly as I pulled the slide back and chambered a round.

They stared at the gun as if hypnotized as I pointed it directly at a spot between the vamp's eyes. I pulled the trigger with the barrel less than an inch from her forehead. There was an explosion of sound and light as the gun discharged. The large slug punched into the flesh and caused her head to snap back.

"Nope. Guns don't really do much damage, but they do pack a nice punch." I punctuated this statement by firing off a few more rounds into the vampire girl's head. "It won't kill them, but firearms are a great tool to have when hunting. They'll be a lot more useful than most of the basic stuff you're taught about. This gun has saved my life several times."

I neglected to mention that, a few months prior, it had been little to no help as I lost two friends in connection to a case I'd been working that had nearly cost me my life as well. The boy's reaction was what I came to expect from most guys. A gleeful look of a child discovering a new toy and can't wait to play with it. Like most men, he was probably going to get the biggest, baddest gun he could find when he got a chance. Something manly. That was, until he had his first scare and was forced to acknowledge it was a dangerous weapon, not a toy. I just hoped no one got hurt in the process.

Cassie looked even more frightened, which was good. Meaning, when she got around to her first firearm, she would be careful, if the fear of it didn't scare her off them altogether. Of the two, she had more potential to survive the longest. Very few vampire hunters live a long time. If they're lucky or unlucky, depending on how you see it, they'll survive just long enough to have families to mourn their deaths. Morbid, but that's the cold, hard truth. They would eventually have to learn that truth for themselves, just as I did at age nine.

I ejected the spent clip and popped a fresh one in before I put the gun back beneath my coat. Both of them were still affixed with my every moment as I bent down and rummaged through my bag. I came back up holding my woodsman's ax. It was a heavy, standard wood chopping ax you can buy at any hardware store. This one had a five-pound head on it. Nice and heavy with good leverage for chopping. I had lost my last ax when a vampire had bitten clear through the steelhead.

"Okay, kids, time to get off the bench and get your hands dirty." I looked at them and held up the ax. "Tell me what you know about the Stake, the Sword, and the Fire."

"The Stake, the Sword, and the Fire is the original method for dispatching vampires created by the head of our Order, Doctor Abraham Van Helsing, in 1897 during the pursuit of a vampire claiming to be Count Vlad Dracul as recorded in the collected journals of Stoker." Cassie rattled off again, sounding as though she'd committed her lessons to memory. "Dr. Helsing was your great-great-grandfather, wasn't he?"

"Yes, when the Helsings immigrated to the U.S. after World War I, their name was changed to Halson by an overworked immigration clerk on Ellis Island." I don't really like to talk about my family history. Belonging to the Helsing family was the Order's version of being a Kennedy. We were legends, even among the legendary vampire hunters.

"Count Dracula wasn't the real Vlad Dracul, just a pretender wannabe with a handful of really freaky vampire powers. You still get vampires claiming to be Dracul every now and then. I've killed a few myself, and you will probably kill a couple."

Cassie straightened. "The events held in the Stoker journals caused the vampire awakening of the twentieth century after science had fooled the West into believing the monsters were just fairy tales. The Order of Helsing was the first such organized order of vampire hunters in Europe. After a disagreement with the emerging German military, who wanted to weaponize vampirism to create the Ü̲berSoldat, super-soldier vampires, the Helsing family left Europe for the States, finding it to be an unpoliced feeding ground for vampires. However, the Helsings, now the Halsons, fought for the Allies to prevent Hitler from unleashing an army of vampires."

"Yeah, yeah, yeah," I interrupted her. "I didn't ask for a family history lesson. I asked about the practice of the Stake, the Sword, and the Fire."

"The practice of the Stake, the Sword, and the Fire is the method of hunting and killing vampires, particularly during the day, as this is the ideal time to assault a vampire while it's asleep," answered Jake.

"Good. Now, have either of you ever actually seen this performed?"

They both shook their heads.

"Well, you're going to get to do it yourselves then."

They stared at me as though I'd just grown an extra nose. Seriously, why did they think they were holding stakes and mallets? I sighed and motioned them forward.

"Now, in an ideal situation," I started, "the vampire is asleep. They don't have to sleep in coffins, though that is traditional and more secure than most other ways." I led them around to each side of the platform. "The function of the Stake is to hold the vampire down. That's all it does. It doesn't kill them, though it does hurt. They don't go *poof* like on TV. This is to hold them down for when you behead and burn them. Jake, go ahead and do it."

I guided him in placing the large wooden stake just to the left of the sternum. It was difficult, given all the chains I'd used to pin the vampire down. Better safe than sorry. Once the stake was in place, Jake raised his mallet and slammed it down onto the head of the stake.

The vampire shrieked as the wood bit into her chest. Jake and Cassie curled back, but I grabbed Jake's arm and forced him to steady the stake.

"You have to be quick and focused. If you don't, then in the field, the vampire could awaken and try to sit up as you're staking it. Never lose focus." I held his gaze with mine.

He nodded and continued pounding in the stake. It took him longer to put in than was good enough for an Order examiner, but I wasn't one. Besides, I found it pointless. As he got a little older and stronger and had some practice, he would be able to stake a vampire in no time flat.

"What you've just done is completely pointless," I told them.

They stared at me in shock.

"Then why did I have to do it?" Jake asked.

"It's tradition, and the Order is big on tradition. But you have to remember this was thought up in 1897 by scared men who were fighting a monster that had been hunting and killing their wives and daughters. Since then, we've made progress and learned more about killing vamps."

The vampire in question had gone still and was fizzing and spitting like a person having a seizure.

"So, next is the Sword?" he said as though it was more of a question.

"Yes, though back in 1897, they actually used large hunting knives that most people carried when traveling in the country. But I guess Sword sounded better than big ass knife. For the sake of argument, we are going to use this." I held up the ax and offered it to Cassie.

She shook her head and stepped away from me.

"This is something you have to do. This is why you came here," I said to the frightened girl.

She finally stepped forward and took the ax. I helped her scramble up on the makeshift dais so she could be in a good position to behead the vampire.

"The Sword refers to beheading the vampire. It severs the vampire's control of its body and powers, neutering it. It doesn't kill a vampire. They can recover if given enough time. This part, like the Stake, won't kill it, nor is it necessary, but it's still very important and something you should do every chance you get, and you won't get many."

I watched Cassie take a deep breath and heft the ax to her shoulder. Then, she raised the ax high above her head, and the vampire let out one last cry as the sharp blade came down on her throat.

It was a single, perfect blow. The head bounced off and went rolling across the ground as gouts of blood spurted from the severed neck.

That was enough for Jake. The young man turned and threw up all over the ground. I will give him points for not puking on the vampire's body.

Cassie let the ax fall from her hands as all the color bled from of her face. She was shaking as she stepped down from the platform. It was hard on a kid for her first time, but they'd been luckier than mine. Their vampire victim hadn't been able to try to eat them.

"Finally, the Fire," I declared, lifting a gas can and dousing the body, glad they no longer had to do anything. "The point of the Stake, the Sword, and the Fire is to subdue the vampire, then burn it, as fire is the only sure way to kill a vampire. The Order wants you to learn the traditional way, but when it comes down to it, it doesn't matter how you get the job done as long as you burn the sucker."

I popped a wooden match alight with my thumbnail and tossed it into the gas fumes. The body exploded in a fireball, shooting flames nearly thirty feet into the sky.

We stood there and watched the body burn for a few moments before I told them they could pack up and beat it. The sun was going to be coming up soon, so I wanted them, and more importantly, me, to be in bed before it was fully daytime. It had been a long night and previous day for me. I had to hunt down and capture the vampire for tonight's little BBQ. I was bushed and just wanted to go to sleep.

Jake and Cassie packed up their tools, not looking at me, and making an effort not to look at each other. There was definitely chemistry between them. They made a cute couple. I knew their lives were only going to get harder from here on out.

As they started off across the abandoned parking lot behind the factory warehouse I called home, I picked up the severed vampire head. Its mouth was still moving in silent screams, even though there were no lungs to give it breath. Small miracles. I tossed the head into the bonfire with the body and watched it all burn.

An apt metaphor for life. Eventually, we all burn.

Chapter 2

The sun was just starting to peek above the horizon as I finally tossed all my tools into the trunk of my beat-up old Plymouth Road Runner. I was tired. All I could think about was dragging my nearly dead body inside the huge warehouse and to bed. I wanted my soft mattress and fluffy pillow so I could sleep the sleep of the dead.

Creepy, I know, but when you're that tired, your brain can get a little morbid.

Then, something happened that pissed me off. My goddamn cell phone rang. This was why I hated cell phones. Too damn convenient, always on, always at hand. It's a complete pain in the ass. I miss the days of missed calls and answering machines. Days when you could just pull out the plug on the phone and say screw it.

The little window popped up showing Alex's office number at the Philadelphia Police Department.

Damn. When she called from her office number, that meant it was official police business. Which, in turn, meant I couldn't blow off her call, even though my finger hovered over the Ignore button.

I sighed and hit Accept to hear the haggard voice of Detective Alex Benson, head of the Philadelphia Special Investigation Case Department, aka the PSIC unit. Lucky me.

"Halson, I need you in my office twenty minutes ago." Her voice sounded grumpy and urgent, yet at the same time, reluctant.

"Well, gee there, detective, let me just jump in my time-traveling Delorean, and I'll be right there." I was prodding the beast, and yes, it was stupid, especially when I was tired. And she was clearly pissed off.

"Don't give me any of your shit, Halson. Just get your scrawny ass over here on the double. I have a problem that needs your expertise." She swore as something crashed in the background.

Alex had been having a hard time over the past few months. She'd watched her partner get brutally killed by a Nosferatu months ago while we were on a case. Then she'd the whole Special Investigations department hoisted onto her shoulders, and the pressure of running an entire underfunded, understaffed, and underappreciated unit was really getting to her. To top it off, we'd been trying to make a go of the couple thing. Granted, we both worked irregular hours, and the foundation of the relationship was built on post-traumatic stress and adrenaline-induced lust.

She was also now pretty much my boss when I consulted for the police in cases that involved vampires, monsters, and other supernatural creatures. The new position had mellowed her out some, and I think she looked sexy with the extra authority.

"Look, I've got a lot on my plate right now. The brass is breathing down my neck to solve this serial killer case, and I need all the help I can get." She sounded even more exhausted than me, and it was only seven in the morning.

"Sorry, babe. You know I'm the guy you call when you have a monster problem. I let you deal with pesky mortals killing each other. It's not really my wheelhouse."

"I've been trying to put this off as long as possible, but it's starting to look like our killer may not be human. I can't go into details over the phone. Get down here as fast as you can so I can bring you up to speed."

I groaned into the phone, making my displeasure very obvious. I really just wanted to go to bed and not wake up for a day or three.

"Halson, I really need you."

I groaned again.

"Oh, and Halson?"

"What?" I huffed into the phone. This was turning into another long and shitty day.

"Have you had breakfast yet?"

"Alex, I haven't even been to bed yet."

"Good, because you don't want to see this on a full stomach."

Well, shit, that didn't sound good. I mentally calculated the time and distance to the PSIC building and back. If I broke every speed limit and possibly the sound barrier, I could get there and be back in about two hours. Three if I factored in an hour for the briefing.

"Fine, I'll be—" I'd spoken before realizing I was talking to an empty line. Alex had hung up on me.

I hated that about her. She would hang up without warning or sound, and I would spend fifteen minutes talking to my hand. I'm pretty sure that's how Jim Gordon feels every time Batman disappears when he turns his back.

I got into my old beat-up car and took a few minutes to bang my head against the steering wheel. Oh, the things I do for love.

An hour later, I was sitting in the cramped PSIC conference room that also served as the combination briefing and interrogation room. I tried to ignore the blood stains on the carpet as I slouched in my oh-so-comfortable folding chair. It had a slightly bent leg, causing it to slant to one side. On the upside, it kept me awake because every time I was about to nod off, I would start to slide off my seat and jerk awake.

The room was small for a conference room and had no windows, which was probably why they used it to beat confessions out of people. The walls were corkboard, which was great for deadening the sound, especially screams of pain, and giving me some probable cause for the bent chair leg. The only other furnishings in the room at the moment were a folding card table on which Benson placed her laptop and a small portable projector.

"What have you heard about the Full Moon Slasher case?" she asked as she set up the computer and started hooking up the projector.

"Honestly, nothing. I haven't really been keeping up with current events lately. Been a bit busy with some Order stuff and getting my new place fully setup." I swirled the paper cup of cop shop sludge they called coffee. I sipped at it a bit and then violently spit out a mouthful. Great. It was basically cold diarrhea in a Dixie cup.

"Don't be such a wimp, Halson." Alex didn't even look up at me from her place under the table as she searched for a power outlet.

I frowned and sat the cup on the edge of the table before reaching over and snatching her warm plastic travel mug. Popping the top, I took a whiff of the steamy brew. Mmm. French vanilla she'd brought from home or had, at least, bought at a coffee shop and smuggled it in. I took a big mouthful and instantly felt my tongue begin to blister from the heat.

Suddenly, the projector's light sprang to life, turning the mostly blank far wall into a flickering movie screen. It would've been an ideal spot, with the exception of the one hole that had been punched into the wall. However, compared to the other walls, it was the best, considering it only had one hole. Seriously, this place was a shit box.

City Hall and the powers that determine which squeaky wheels get greased didn't see fit to waste money on frills for the PSIC. Apparently, they had faith in the cops under Alex's command's abilities to keep suspects from tunneling out of the building, something you could do with only a slice of cheese and a strong cough. Most of the false ceiling tiles were missing, and many of the fluorescent light fixtures were replaced with singular naked lightbulbs.

The projector light flickered again, and a high-resolution image appeared. High-resolution is not one of those things you really want when being shown murder scene photos. The scene in the picture was like something out of a horror movie from the seventies. It was a shot of what looked like someone's living room. There was a large couch with a matching recliner. Both were lying overturned on the floor. The large entertainment center was off kilter as one lower corner had been smashed, so it all leaned to one side. It hadn't fully fallen over because the upper corner had snagged on the far wall, keeping it propped up. The TV had spilled out of its cubby hole and landed on the floor, face down. I could see shards of glass that had probably been the TV screen.

Knick-knacks and the kind of flotsam that accumulates in well-lived homes were strewn across the floor, in most cases, smashed and broken. It was hard to see the things that represented the parts of someone's life destroyed like that. It stirred up deeply buried feelings and made old scars ache. It was violent, obvious there had been a serious struggle, and it was clear it had not ended well for someone because there was blood everywhere.

There was just so much red. Blood covered everything. It wasn't like someone had gotten injured, a serious injury, the kind that bleeds everywhere and requires emergency life-saving operations and hours of prayers. No, it was like whoever it came from had simply just exploded. It coated almost every inch of the floor and was sprayed up the walls. What body parts I could discern among the carnage could've fit in my pocket.

"These photos don't show it, but blood and body parts are even on the ceiling," Alex said, addressing my stunned, slack-jawed state. "That is all from just one victim. The second we found in the bedroom."

My stomach did a lurching flop as my brain tried to reconstruct all that gore into a single human being. Whatever had attacked him had been strong, angry, and brutal. No human could've done that to another person.

There was a click, and the slide changed to show another room. It was decorated the same as the first, with smashed furniture and far too much gore. This picture was centered on the bed. Its heavy wood headboard was pressed up against the wall and shattered as if by an incredible impact. In the center of the impact point was the mostly intact, slumped body of what could've been a woman. It was hard to tell since most of her torso had been torn open, and her insides lay in her lap. She was covered in blood so much that even her hair had been soaked, and it had become a lank and stringy mass the color of rust.

"Why was she not torn apart like the other one?" I asked.

"We don't know, but from the coroner's report, whatever killed her took the heart."

We both gave that a thought for a moment. Whatever was strong enough to reduce a person to a pulp and gut another like a fish took the heart for a reason other than food.

"What about the other one, the victim that was torn apart in the living room," I asked. If the heart was missing too, it could be mystical, in which case I could pack up and go home since I don't do magic.

"Unknown, since we could only identify about a fourth of what we could find," Alex said, double-checking her notes. "However, in the other six cases, at least one victim was missing a heart that we know of. Every other scene has the same MO, gore, and destruction, and of the complete victims we could find, all were missing hearts. Of the other eight victims, all were torn into bits so small, some of the bodies are not yet identified. How much do you know about this case?"

"Well, I told you I haven't been really following it. For the most part, I haven't even been watching the news. But I do know that it's been a pretty big deal in the media."

Alex sighed. I get the impression that my whimsical nature sometimes irks her.

"This first murder was almost three weeks ago, on the first night of the full moon." She clicked her laptop's touchpad, and the picture changed again. The same scene, new location. Blood and guts everywhere, and another gutted body. "This took place the next night and then the third." Another, and the nightmare continued in different home. "This time, it was a whole family with kids."

I couldn't look anymore, and turned away from the wall. A family with kids murdered by a monster was too close to home for me, and I had to put my head between my knees until the static in my skull stopped. The images of the dead kids? I couldn't even begin to describe it, but the emotions that had blazed in me had been too much. There was something so much worse about murdered children, about the loss of their innocent lives. They shouldn't have to worry about things like monsters and death. They should be running around outside, climbing trees, and laughing in the sunlight.

Now, they would never get to grow up and suffer the pangs of first love or the pain of losing that love. They would never have their own families and raise their own children. The only kindness in that horror was that none of them would be burdened with having to live with what had happened to their loved ones or having to witness it. I knew too well the weight of survivor's guilt.

"Then, for the next three days, there was nothing. There were no more murder scenes. The killer just stopped. So, the media called them the Full Moon Killings, and their so-called professionals estimated there would be more killings at the next full moon."

"That is a little presumptuous on their part. Three murders that just happen to be on the nights of the full moon are a coincidence, not a pattern. Maybe if it had happened at least two months in a row, but this is getting way ahead of themselves," I said.

"Well, coincidence doesn't sell news stories. Serial killers with patterns sell stories. As if Philadelphia didn't have enough problems with gang violence, drug wars, and the mob's leftovers, they have to go and invent a serial killer for ratings." She fumed.

"Damn liberal media," I said in mock outrage, trying to make a joke and ease myself back into a calmer state of mind.

Alex leaned forward on her elbows, her hands clasped to her temples as if to keep her brains from bursting out of her skull.

"Well, they were right and wrong. Four nights later, our killer got stuck again. This time on a night without a full moon, with only one victim whose heart was torn out." She gestured at a set of photos showing a dirty motel room decorated in crimson splatters where some down-on-his-luck guy got mauled. It was less gory than the rest, but to be fair, the killer only had one victim's worth of blood to work with. "The next night, the same thing happened. This time, it was a little old couple in their kitchen, then he stopped. Randomly, it starts up a couple of nights later. There is no pattern as to when or why he kills these people. None of them are connected. None of them knew each other, all at random times and places."

"Maddening," I agreed, trying to commiserate with her. I was afraid she was about to start tearing out her hair by the handful. "But from what I've seen so far, I don't even begin to know what to tell you. All I can say is whatever it is, it's big, strong, and insanely pissed off. As far as the hearts go, I don't know of anything that would only eat the heart without eating everything else, and since they are taking hearts from all the victims, that seems like it would be a ritual. I'm not a magic guy, so I can't help in that department." That got me an exasperated look, which I tried to buffer with one of my oafish grins.

"There is one thing we've kept from the reporters so far." Alex brought up a new file and put it on the screen. "We found it at the scene of the third murder on the last night of the full moon."

The picture was a dedicated shot showing a single piece of evidence. It was a bloody paw print. I stood up and approached the screen on the wall for a better look. Even when my shadow blocked out part of the image projection, I couldn't take my eyes off what I saw.

It looked like a dog's paw print, only it was slightly elongated and much, much bigger. Next to the print, some CSI had laid an evidence ruler. They are used in crime scene photos to give perspective and show the size of evidence in the picture. The rulers showed twelve-inch markings and were placed below and along the print to show width and length. It was nearly fourteen inches long, a foot wide, and it was a wolf's print.

Your average North American timber wolf track is about four to five inches long and three to four inches wide. This paw print was nearly three or four times that size. The typical wolf weighs up to seventy-five pounds, stands about two to three feet at the shoulder, and can reach nearly six feet in length. They were the premier apex predator in the US before settlers hunted them into near extinction. Wolves are extremely badass. They can run at nearly twenty-five miles an hour over long distances. Their noses were sensitive enough to track better than some bloodhounds, and they had night vision. Their jaws are strong enough to crush a human skull, and they are full of fangs that can slice through flesh like Ginsu knives.

Try imagining all that in a package nearly twice that size and fueled by pure rage. The creature that had left this print had been over six feet at the shoulder and weighed over three hundred pounds of lean muscle. More than powerful enough to have caused all the carnage in the photos, and I did not want to cross paths with it.

"The CSIs couldn't ID the print. The closest thing they can say is it looks like a wolf. Calculations of the print put it at just over one hundred eighty centimeters in height and well over one hundred thirty-six kilos." Alex echoed my thoughts almost exactly. The metric confused me. I'm a strong believer in the American standard system, mainly because I'm too lazy and idiotic to learn to convert. "That is a *big* freaking wolf."

"Oh, it's worse than you think," I added. "These wolves are bipedal, making our killer well over nine feet tall. Pretty average as far as werewolves go, though."

"Did you just say werewolf?" Alex asked, as though she couldn't believe we were having this conversation.

"Yeah, werewolf. From the German, meaning man-wolf, I think, though my German sucks. I thought that was why you called me in."

"Well, yeah, but it just sounds weird when you say it out loud like that."

We looked at each other and shared that nearly telepathic notion our lives were getting a little too weird for our liking. Alex leaned forward on her desk again, bringing us closer, and in the bad mixed lighting of the police station, it made her look even more gorgeous than usual. She was a blonde goddess with a long, slim-waisted body that was hard and well-toned from daily trips to the gym. I had seen her nearly naked once, and trust me when I tell you, her body is the definition of perfection. She had been straddling me at the time and desperately wanted to rock my world and my bed. I had almost let her because I had really, really, really wanted to.

Thankfully, after years of meditation and being a good-hearted guy with a weak spot for women in need, I had been able to wrestle down both of our overclocked libidos. We escaped that night without making any rash decisions, with our friendship and my virginity intact. Yes, I am a virgin. Nearly thirty, and still a virgin. My love life was one of the many casualties of my line of work. Not the stuff you use to try to recruit people to your cause.

"So, what do you know about werewolves," she asked, still looking as if she couldn't believe she was having this conversation. "Silver bullets, full moons, and pentagrams on the palm of the hand? What do we do?" She started to get that panicky lilt to her voice, probably having flashbacks to the last and her first encounter with a supernatural monster that had tried to kill us both. The encounter had left her with a small white scar on the left side of her mouth. Though the emotional and psychological scars were a lot deeper and nastier, she was dealing with it the best she could.

"Well, lycanthropes are basically people infected with the beastial spirits of rage, according to German lore. During the full moon, the spirit grows so strong that it takes over the person's body and transforms them into a bloodthirsty monster of pure rage. They can't control it. And they generally have no memory of what happens when they are in beast form. In animal form, they have all the strengths and abilities of a wolf, increased by their size and supernatural powers." I leaned back in my chair and put my boots up on her desk with my hands behind my head as I tried to remember what I could about werewolves.

"How do we kill them, silver bullets?" she asked.

"Well, yeah, but it's not easy because they can heal nearly all mortal wounds. Silver doesn't kill them. Supposedly, because it's considered "Moon Metal" or something, but more like they have an allergy to it, and their healing can't work while wounded with silver. Fire also works because, like with vampires, it burns them away faster than they can heal. I've heard decapitation can kill them." I pretty much exhausted my store of knowledge.

"You Order guys love to chop the heads off things, don't you?"

"We are a simple bunch," I agreed.

"Okay, so how do we find this werewolf?" She kept pumping me for answers as if she thought I was some sort of preternatural Wikipedia just for her use.

"I dunno, the Yellow Pages maybe. Listed under W for wolf, or would it be W for were?" I tend to rely on my wit in times of crisis, especially when I don't have answers.

Alex frowned at me.

"I have no clue. Unlike Hollywood and TV, there is no real way to tell if someone is a werewolf shy of going on a stroll with them during a full moon. Camouflage is how supernatural creatures have survived for thousands of years, and that doesn't work well when people can see through it."

She gave a frustrated huff and crossed her arms over her chest. I won't deny it did wonderful things to her breasts that caused my train of thought to derail.

"So, we can't find this thing until it kills again, and there is no way to track it." Alex pondered more to herself than to me.

"Well, that's what's bothering me." She gave me a puzzled look, so I explained. "A werewolf only transforms during a full moon, which makes sense for your first three nights, which were on the nights of the full moon. But all these other kills happened much later, on nights when the moon wasn't full." I looked through the notes on Alex's desk for the dates of the other attacks to confirm.

Alex slammed her hand down on top of the papers and glared at me. "Halson, please stop shooting holes in our only lead. This case has been one huge shitstorm, and I'm getting shit on from so high up that it freezes on the way down. I *need* to solve this case as soon as possible because there is a lot of politics and media riding on this, not to mention my job." She spoke through gritted teeth, causing a bit of spit to fly when she talked. I could see the stress this was putting on her.

"Fine, Al. I will look around to see what I can do on it and maybe make a call or two, okay?" Consoling her probably would have worked better had I not used the pet name I had for her. She hated it, but I couldn't resist. I loved teasing her. "They won't really fire you, will they?"

"I don't know," she replied, looking as exhausted as I felt. "But if someone's head has to roll for this, it will probably be mine. The heads of the department are not happy with the Special Investigation unit, especially after what happened with

Bullard's death, and they didn't want me to get the job in the first place. I was just the only one with any real experience."

That made me feel rotten because it had been partially my fault, and because of me, Bullard had gotten killed. I had nearly gotten Alex killed, too. And she had gotten her first, real, undeniable look at the monsters.

She had been dealing with the shock better than most people. The world at large chooses to ignore the monsters and supernatural parts of the world. Even those idiot ghost and monster hunters, when faced with the truth, turn a blind eye and pretend it doesn't exist. People will go to any lengths to deny it, mainly because people do not like the idea that they are not at the top of the food chain and that there might be monsters out there that can eat them. It's easier to close your eyes and tell yourself the boogeyman is not in your closet, that there are no monsters under your bed, and nothing can hurt you as long as you are under the covers, but the world isn't like that.

Bullard's death hit her pretty hard, but she'd managed to pull herself together, at least for appearance's sake. Her guard was up at all times now, and it has been a bit difficult to get close to her after that first time. Neither of us tried to push the intimacy of sex, and both of us had our personal hang-ups. The scar on her mouth wasn't the only one she received from her encounter with the Nosferatu. Keeping those kinds of emotional wounds buried wouldn't help them heal, but I don't have the social skills to begin to help her.

Alex had put on her tough cop face and embraced the danger. She had been fun and playful before, while we still had our repartee and banter, but now there was an icy edge to everything. Even when we just hung out, she was still holding me at arm's length. To be fair, I did the same with her. I had never been close to anyone after my family's deaths, and now, with Alex, it was hard and still a little awkward.

"Okay, okay, okay," I said, breaking down under her stern look. "I promise to look around and see what I can turn up, but it's going to cost you extra."

She smiled. "Pizza and beer, my place?"

"Let's make it my place, and I feel like Chinese tonight. Oh, and please leave all your gory and brutal police work at the office. I already have enough nightmare material without you adding to it."

"Deal." She finally relaxed and turned off the projector.

I couldn't bear to look at any more of those horrible scenes. I could still see the carnage when I closed my eyes. I was going to see it in my dreams tonight. One of the reasons Alex and I hadn't made love or even slept over at one another's place. I woke up every night screaming from night terrors, and that's not really something people want to sleep next to. I'm also afraid of how she would react to it or how it would color her opinion of me. Hard to portray yourself as a big, tough, macho man after a woman has seen you crying and screaming like a child.

Alex looked for her coffee mug for the first time, realizing it was missing. She glared at me when she saw I'd been drinking from it. I gave her my big arrogant asshole grin as I finished off the coffee and sat the mug on her desk. She continued to give me a murderous glare as she took my rejected cup of nasty station coffee and shotgunned the entire thing in a single swig without wincing.

Damn, that was hardcore. I should really be careful around her. She could probably hurt me.

She kicked me out of the police station, saying she would stop by after she got off work. I turned up the collar on my duster. The heavy canvas took most of the bite out of the cold wind.

Now, in addition to training a couple of kids, I had to deal with a possible serial killer werewolf. I was starting to feel like

I was in a Laurell K. Hamilton novel, minus all the sex and strippers.

I slid into the Road Runner's driver seat and turned the wrench to start the car. The key had snapped off in the ignition several weeks ago and I'd just clamped an old wrench to the stub. It seemed the easiest solution at the time. Not a lot of auto places still make keys for vehicles from the 60s. As it roared to life, I banged on the dashboard until the heater finally kicked on and started to blow out lukewarm air. It wasn't much, but it would make the long drive home bearable as I tried to think of ways to track a werewolf.

Chapter 3

I n the hour it took me to drive home, the light flurries of flakes had turned into a blizzard that blew sideways. I drove hunched over the steering wheel, alternately punching the dash every few minutes to keep the barely functioning heater going. It wasn't much, but it kept me from freezing my ass off. I cursed constantly and wished I had just ignored Alex's call. I could've been home safe and warm, sleeping in my bed.

I finally managed to pull into the empty lot of an abandoned factory warehouse that served as my home. It had been some old machine factory at one time, and whatever company it had been had left behind a large warehouse and a bunch of machining tools. I considered it a huge windfall as it saved me a lot of expenses in the upkeep of my equipment. I had bought the property at a steal of a price during a liquidation auction, turning it into my own personal base of operations.

I hit the remote clipped to my sun visor, activating one of the roll-up loading bay doors to open. This allowed me to drive past the smoldering remains of the plinth fire where we had burned the vampire and up a short ramp into the building itself. Once inside, I activated the door again, sending it back down the track and closed. From the outside, the lot would look abandoned again. This was a great way to hide from people or things that you might not want to find you.

The interior of the building was mostly just an open floor, with columns placed evenly throughout for support. The centermost section was surrounded by a giant fence-like structure. It looked like a massive version of those battle cages wrestlers or MMA fighters use. I built it out of scavenged parts from the local scrapyard and some welding equipment that had been left in the building. It had cost surprisingly little and was extremely strong for something poorly designed and built by an amateur with no clue what he was doing. There was no such thing as too much security when your profession is killing creatures that can crush a car like a beer can.

Inside this monster cage was what looked like a mismatched number of TV sets randomly pieced together. This was what served as my apartment. It was a rather spacious studio area with a living room, dining room, and kitchen. Most of the furnishings were second or third-hand from Goodwill and thrift shops. In the back was a combination workroom and armory where I stored and repaired any equipment. I have no clue what they had made in the building, but they had left all kinds of machines and equipment here. I had everything from welding equipment to heavy milling machines. I could manufacture almost anything.

Outside the cage, behind my "apartment," I'd set up a small shooting range. I practice every day and even have my own reloading setup for making my own bullets. This was going to come in handy now that I needed to run off a batch of silver bullets, but I would do that tomorrow. Right now, I wanted to fall face down on my bed and pass out.

My bedroom was just a loft over the living room. I built it so that the bed sunk into the loft floor. It's a California king-size mattress with about two feet of walking space all around it and a guard rail surrounding the entire loft, just in case. I needed a large bed I couldn't just roll out of. I toss and turn a lot in my sleep and used to fall out of bed a lot when I was younger until I just started sleeping on the floor. It's super soft and comfy, though big enough for several people to sleep in.

I unlocked the heavy gate on the cage that served as my front door and stepped into my apartment. And a man was sitting on my couch.

"Oh God, not you." I groaned.

Gillette sat on my couch, his long legs stretched out in front of him with his boots propped on my coffee table, and he was playing my Xbox. Don't get me wrong, Gillette was probably my best and only friend, and it's not like I hate the guy, but I totally hate the guy. He's six feet tall and model handsome. He wore his dirty blond hair long. Not as long as mine, but infinitely more stylish. He dressed equally as stylish and always looked like he had just stepped off a fashion runway in Milan or Paris.

We shared the same goofy, asshole attitude, and that was probably part of the reason why we got along so much better than other people, but it also got on my nerves a lot as well. When around him and on the receiving end for a change, I could see why people sometimes got irritated with me. He also always had money, cars, and women. And routinely flaunted it around and rubbed it in my face. Even with all that, the thing that really made me hate him was the fact he's a wizard.

I hate magic with a passion. Like most people, I don't really like the fact that someone out there can just reach out with it and kill me from anywhere at any time, and there was no way to guard against it. It's unnerving, and unless you've seen a wizard such as Gillette really cut loose with a major display of destructive magic, you really don't have a perspective for the kinds of things they can do. And Gillette was one of the most powerful wizards in the world.

When most people think wizard, they think Gandalf or Dumbledore. Old guy with a long white beard and robes, but Gillette looked and dressed like a rockstar. He wore nearly form-fitting black leather pants, with a matching black tank top showing off his toned upper body. The shirt was too small and looked painted onto his chest. He had the slim, muscular build of someone who lifted weights, but not to excess. I'm not that bad myself, but my build is more starved laborer than fitness model.

"Hey, get your feet off my table, you animal." I snarled, sitting down next to him.

He left his black designer engineer boots right where they were. His hands glittered with large silver rings, each studded with a different colored stone. There was one on each of his fingers, ten in all, and a couple of bracelets dangling from his wrists. The jewelry looked gaudy as hell, but I knew they were not for decoration. Each one was a powerful magical talisman he used to harness powerful spells. I'd seen him use them to shoot fire and lightning from his hands. The experience had been terrifying, but he'd saved my life more than once.

"Hey!" Gillette exclaimed as I took the Xbox controller away from him. He punched me in the shoulder, and the rings made it hurt like hell. I let out a roar and hit him back, making it hurt him as much as his punch hurt me. I don't have big, clunky rings, but years of hitting a heavy bag had made my knuckles hard and bony.

"Damn, mate, what is your problem?" He winced a bit and rubbed his shoulder.

Did I mention Gillette had a British accent? Yeah, women eat that sort of thing up, but it was just another thing about him that annoyed me.

"Serious problems, man. The Order has me training some new kids. On top of that, Alex just brought me on board to a really serious serial killer case, which we think may be the work of a werewolf, and I've had no sleep in the last twenty-four hours. I'm completely done in." I sighed and slumped lower on the couch. My eyelids were starting to droop.

"I saw your bonfire and was wondering what you guys were doing out there." Gillette took the controller back from my sleep-impaired hands.

"You've been here since last night? What the hell were you doing, just sitting here playing games the whole time?" I growled. Boy, that pissed me off. He was always pulling shit like that.

"No, I was also drinking your shitty American beer." There were several empty bottles sitting next to his end of the couch and a few lying on the floor.

I groaned. I really was not in the mood and didn't have the energy to put up with his crap right now. I just wanted my bed and sleep. Gillette leaned over and burped loudly into my ear. His breath smelled awful.

"I really can't deal with this right now, man. I am wrecked and need some sleep. I'll talk to you tomorrow." I let out another moan and managed to stagger to my feet. The caffeine from earlier was finally wearing off, and I was about to crash hard.

"G'night, mate," Gillette called after me.

"Get out," I shot over my shoulder, and he just laughed. I shrugged off my heavy duster and left it lying on the floor at the base of the spiral stairs that led up to my loft bed. I kicked my boots and socks off as I climbed the stairs, leaving them where they fell. At the top, I stripped off my shoulder holster and shirt.

And the gun I tossed into the bed. The rig and shirt I dropped at the foot of the bed, along with my arm knives and other assorted equipment that had been in my pockets. My cell phone I sat on the little side table I'd made out of a crate, where I had a reading lamp and a few paperback Jim Butcher novels.

I rolled onto the big soft mattress where something hard and painful poked me in the back. I pulled the 1911 out from under me and shoved it under my pillow. Yeah, it was a little 80's action movie-ish, but it got the job done. My back gave another twinge, so I rolled onto my stomach and buried my face in a pillow. Pulling the thick, heavy blanket over my head, I finally drifted off into the warm darkness of sleep.

Chapter 4

My dreams were a disjointed mess, with incoherent scenes featuring oceans of blood, hungry fanged mouths, and tearing meat. Unseen primal beasts hunted me in my nightmares, trying to devour me whole. Thankfully, I was saved from this horrible fate by waking to the delicious smells of food cooking, a far better wake-up call than my usual method of screaming myself awake.

I pulled a tank top on, having not removed my pants from this morning. A quick glance at my cell showed some time after four to six hours of sleep, new personal best. Most nights, I woke three or four times screaming from night terrors. A life like mine lead to a very colorful palate for my brain to draw from and torture me with.

The smell of grease and cooking foods floated up to my loft. It smelled like bacon, eggs, and coffee. Thoughts of delicious, hot foodstuffs made my mouth water. I nearly tripped on my way down the stairs to find Gillette in my little kitchen area cooking up a storm. He had transformed it into something out of a fairytale.

There were literal piles of food stacked on my table—onions, peppers, slabs of bacon, and mounds of real coffee beans. Actual strands of linked sausages hung from a pan rack with strings of garlic cloves. Gillette himself was standing at my stove, which had actual fire shooting from the top. My stove is electric. Each burner had a hot cast iron pan sitting on its own corona of flame, spitting hot melted fat and grease.

It smelled wonderful, but there was a major problem with it all. It was magic.

I *hate* magic. I cannot state that enough. There was no one real reason. You just can't trust it. Magic was terrifying. There's nothing a magic user cannot do with it. With it, they can make you see and feel things that aren't real, and the real kicker is what they can destroy with it. Yeah, if they wished, wizards of Gillette's standard can call down lightning and fire from the sky to wipe anything off the face of the earth that displeases them, but that's all just for show. I know if some of the more powerful magic users had half a mind, they could just blink and, *poof*, you're dead.

It's terrifying to think someone could just slap the life out of you with a mere thought from the other side of the planet. So, I regard it with suspicion, and while the food looked good, it could all very well have been an elaborate illusion. It would be just Gillette's sense of humor to conjure up fake food and make it all disappear, leaving me munching on thin air.

Did I mention he was an asshole?

Tentatively, I approached the coffee pot and prodded it with the handle of a wooden spoon. It seemed real enough, so I poured myself a cup and took a sip. It was amazing. There was no need for cream or sugar. This was real coffee, from fresh ground beans, put through a French press. I eyed the plates sitting on the table stacked with bacon, fried eggs, homemade county gravy, and from-scratch biscuits.

"Well, go on, it's not gonna bite you," Gillette called from his place at the stove.

Flames jumped and licked the wall and ceiling, yet it didn't leave scorch marks. Apparently, whatever magic spell he was casting on my stove was all an illusion to make it look more impressive. I had seen what he could do with fire, and the last time had ended with several slagged cars and a burning fire hydrant. I glared in suspicion at the food, and Gillette sighed.

He left his station at the stove and moved over to the table where a black doctor's bag sat.

He plunged both arms into the bag, up almost to his shoulders. You know that scene in *Mary Poppins* where she takes the lamp and hat rack out of her handbag? Yeah, Gillette's magic bag worked pretty much the same way. I have no clue how much stuff it can hold or how much is in there, but it seems whatever he needs just pops out. Honestly, it genuinely freaks me out.

"Ah right, plate up," Gillette exclaimed, pulling out several plates and some silverware. He handed me one, and I took it.

"It's real food, not magic, I swear," he confirmed when he saw me still looking at the food apprehensively.

I gave him a hard glare before deciding to trust him and dug in. I piled my plate with bacon, eggs, sausage, and biscuits, then slathered the entire thing in rich white gravy. The next ten minutes were spent shoveling food into my mouth and chasing it with a hot mouthful of coffee. It burned, but was totally worth it. Everything tasted amazing. The gravy was rich, the biscuits flaky, and the bacon crispy.

Grease dripped down my chin, but it had been so long since I'd had a good, hot, home-cooked meal. My breakfast usually consisted of cold leftovers or bad coffee, if at all, so I was getting my fill before Gillette made it all go *poof*. The entire time, I kept one eye on him as I ate. He just kept cooking, piling up more and more food. There was no way in hell I was gonna be able to eat it all, but I was going to try my best.

Twenty minutes later, I gave up, sitting back in my chair to unbutton my pants. I couldn't have eaten another bite, and my stomach was upset, protesting the sudden deluge of food after the prolonged rationing of past years. I had barely made a dent in the mountain of food still sitting on the table and had no idea what Gillette planned to do with the rest. There would be leftovers for days, not that I was complaining.

"You look fat and happy," Gillette said, waving his hand to dismiss the magic spells he had cast on my kitchen. The raging inferno on my stove disappeared, leaving behind dully glowing burners. The sunlight streaming into the kitchen I hadn't noticed vanished as if someone had snapped a light off. Even the smells became more muted than they had been.

"You know you're cleaning up this mess, right?" I groaned while trying to stand.

"What are you on about? I cooked this lot. The least you can do is the dishes."

"Hell no, you broke into my house and drank my beer. You are lucky I don't shoot you."

"Fair enough. One spotless kitchen, coming up. You want me to dust under the couch, too?" He raised both hands as if conducting an invisible choir, and I nearly jumped out of my skin.

"Oh, hell no, none of that sorcerer's apprentice crap. It didn't turn out too great for Micky," I interrupted before he could explode my place over eight city blocks.

"Micky was an amateur. I am Gillette, the greatest and most wise Magus." He waggled his hands to both sides of his face for dramatic effect.

Now, in his defense, he was pretty amazing when slinging fire and lighting, but he also tends to create a lot of collateral damage.

"Nope, sorry, Harry Potter, you gotta do it like the rest of us muggles."

His face fell as I shot him down, and he stuck out his tongue at me, but he did start gathering up plates and dumping their contents into his little black bag. Once he scraped the plate clean, he just dumped it into the bag as well. I gave up and went off to get some work done before he could cause more trouble.

By work, I meant running off a few hundred silver bullets. That's not how it sounds. You can't make a bullet out of solid silver. It's too soft a metal for that. They tend to warp and are not ballistically stable. Their lightweight tends to subject them to the forces of physics more than good old lead. So, instead of making bullets out of solid silver, you take regular old hollow points and fill the cavity with molten silver, creating a silver-tipped sabot round.

This has two effects. It gives you the benefits of a silver weapon against those nasty beasties that have aversions to it. It also holds the bullet together. Normally, a hollow point flowers out and breaks off, causing damage at the cost of penetration power. These super damaging channels are the selling point for it as a self-defense ammo. Kinda pointless on the supernatural creatures, as most of them have super healing factors that put Wolverine to shame. The silver tip holds the bullet together, keeping its penetration power, so it hits with a lot more force, and even the thickest-skinned or armored boogeymen feel it. Once that silver is in their bodies, it kills their healing.

This is also why I was tipping and hand-loading up 9mm bullets instead of my usual .45 bullets, as power was not as important in this case as volume. With the smaller rounds, I would swap out my 1911 for my Beretta 92f, with the extended box magazines, which held twenty rounds as opposed to the eight rounds the 1911 held. This way, I would be able to pour bullets into my target until they went down. Preternatural creatures, more or less, still have to play by the same rules as us mortals. And when you take away their advantages, they are generally weaker than regular creatures due to the handicap of always having to rely on their superpowers.

Even Gillette was, as far as I knew, a straight-up mortal if you ignored the fact he could bend the forces of nature to his whim. His magic spells and tools made him harder than normal mortals to kill, but I'm pretty sure heart disease or some STD would be the death of him. For hunting were-creatures and other shapeshifters, you just hit them with silver and do as much damage as you can until they wear out. I do wonder if Gillette ever flipped sides, that I would be able to bring him down because currently, my only plans were about how to run away. Who says you can't learn things from *Monty Python*?

After the silver tips had cooled, I hand-loaded them into casings, and had just shy of nine hundred rounds. I tested the new run by firing off some in the range I'd set up out behind the main part of my home. It had been set up just for this purpose. Hand-making your own ammo is very helpful when you may have to create something new to deal with monsters. It's also cheaper when you have to stay on a very low budget, which is always a good thing.

When I finally had the presence of mind to look up from my work, it was almost seven. Meaning, if she didn't get caught up with any new cases, Alex would be here soon. I hurried to finish up and jumped into the shower, wanting to be clean and tidy up following Gillette's invasion of my home.

By seven, I had managed to shower and forgone shaving, deciding to go for the roguish stubble look. I did, however, pull on a clean shirt. I mean, I should put in some effort, considering Alex was out of my league. We had been doing the date night thing for several months. Neither one of us dared to take it any further than movies and dinner. The food was always takeout, but the movies depended on whose choice it was. I usually went for older classics, like black and white Hitchcock films, while Alex always had us watching some dumb buddy cop movie full of action and half naked muscly men like Stallone or Schwarzenegger.

I paused on my way through the kitchen to find it spotless. Gillette had kept his word and cleaned up rather well. There wasn't even any lingering odor of earlier culinary bombardment. I checked the fridge, hoping to see mountains of leftovers, but sadly, it seemed even emptier than usual. I guess he'd magicked away the food along with the mess. Too bad he hadn't done the same with himself.

Gillette was slumped on my couch, watching a channel I'm pretty sure my basic cable package doesn't get. It wasn't porn, although I wouldn't put it past him to have been watching it. That's the kind of thing he would do. It was a soccer game, and it was being broadcast in a foreign language.

"You cannot still be here." I groaned.

"What? Not like I got somewhere else to be. Besides, there's a footy match on."

"Please, for the love of whatever gods you worship, just vanish. For at least a few hours. Alex is coming over so we can eat and watch a movie."

"Ooh, hot date with the girlfriend." He grinned, showing me every single one of his dazzling white teeth. "Sounds like fun. Is she bringing food?"

"Yes, but not for you." I ground my teeth together. The last thing I wanted right now was to have to introduce Alex to this pretty boy sex maniac.

There was a sudden loud buzzing that nearly caused the vein in my forehead to explode.

My front-ish door has a wired intercom and a camera. It allows people to announce themselves and permits me to check them out before remotely releasing the front lock so they can get in. It was a holdover from whatever the factory had been before. Alex had a key, but was polite enough to always ring so I would know when she was coming or going. In addition to being something polite, normal people do, it also kept us from accidentally shooting each other.

That buzz meant she was standing right outside, probably sliding her key into the lock as I furiously tried to think of a way to get a wizard to leave my home voluntarily.

"Please!" I hissed at him.

"Nope," he replied, putting his feet on the coffee table and hunkering in, preparing to make my life hell. I had a moment of blinding panic where I thought of just shooting him. Worst case scenario, dead body on my couch that I could easily cover with a duvet and a few throw pillows, if I had those things. Oddly enough, my place was filled with ways to get rid of a body, just not hide a body.

"Hey, Halson, you know you could give me a hand with these," Alex said as she shouldered open the heavy cage door.

Well, *screwed now*, I thought and reached behind her to hold the metal door. Its weight and the fact I never oiled it made the door a chore to open and close. I always kinda treated it like light exercise, but Alex had plastic bags with small food containers in both hands.

She shuffled past me to the island counter, which separated the kitchen nook from the living room. As she sorted everything onto the counter, unaware of Gillette and talking nonstop, I just stood silently by the door and waited for the bomb to drop. This was going to be messy. Both Alex and Gillette have excess of personality, but both are very different. Whereas Alex was more authority and commanding, Gillette's a lot more like me, a puckish rogue with a disdain for "the man." And Alex was indeed "the man." This was going to be fun to watch from the outside.

She seemed to realize something was wrong and slowly turned to look at me with a slightly inquisitive expression. I'm not usually so quiet, especially when there is food involved. Her curious and rather bossy nature had picked up on this, almost like she was a police detective or something. She raised an eyebrow, and in response, I signaled towards the couch with my eyes. In a blur of motion you would've missed if you hadn't been looking for it, she turned and drew her weapon. Her Glock was leveled at Gillette's head, and he looked as if he'd been expecting it the whole time.

"Oh no, please don't shoot, officer. I'm unarmed," he said in the most bored voice I could have imagined.

"Who the hell are you?" Alex asked, keeping the gun pointed at the end of his nose.

Gillette rose to his feet and stuck out his heavily ringed hand to her. "I'm the amazingly wonderful, all-powerful, never-failing sex god and wizard extraordinaire, but you, my lovely lady of the law, may call me Gillette."

Alex just looked at him as if she couldn't believe what he'd just said.

"He is not serious, is he?" she asked.

"Well, he is a wizard. The rest of it is all delusion," I answered.

"So, why is he here?"

"Mainly because I can't figure out how to get rid of him. Wizards and cockroaches are nearly impossible to get rid of."

"You guys, I'm right here, and you're kinda hurting my feelings." Gillette waved his arms in the air in a comical effort, trying to get our attention and stop ignoring him.

"Have you just tried this?" Alex reached out, grabbed Gillette by his left ear, and dragged him out the cage door.

I stood back and sighed as I watched her continue to drag him across the factory floor to the door she'd come in through. Once there, she flung it open and hurled him bodily through the door and headfirst out into the snow. She slammed the door and locked it. The sound of the lock snapping shut echoed through the empty building. Alex triumphantly marched back with a smile on her face.

"See, Halson, that's how you handle annoying uninvited house guests."

"Really? I don't know why I never thought of that. You might want to check the couch, though, tough guy."

Alex, confused, turned to see Gillette sitting on the couch where he had been before, feet up on the coffee table and everything.

"How—"

"Magic!" Gillette waved his hands on both sides of his face in a parody of jazz hands to emphasize his point.

Alex looked at me in disbelief. "So, he really is a—"

"Wizard, yeah, otherwise I would have chucked him out of here long ago."

"I thought you were kidding about wizards when you mentioned it earlier."

"I wish," I groaned, taking a container of lo mein from the counter and plopping down on the couch next to Gillette.

Alex perched herself on the arm of the couch so she could still see Gillette. "So, what other tricks does he do?"

"I dunno, I'm not even sure if he's even housebroken."

"Okay, I am *right here*. You don't have to talk like I'm not in the room or I'm a dog," Gillette called through a mouthful of food. One of the food containers had magically found its way into his hand. "So, what movie are we watching?"

"Well, *we* were gonna watch Gilda," I answered, noticing the sudden disappearance of my Chinese food.

"Oh, classic Rita Hayworth at her sexiest," he commented.

"I know, right? When she shakes out all that red hair and says, 'Hi, boys.'" I took back my container from Gillette in time to save at least half my food.

"Ugh, how are you two the most unmanly men on the planet?" Alex asked, clearly disappointed we didn't live up to her expectations of grunting and crotch scratching.

We both gave her eye rolls as the movie started.

We continued to eat and watch the film. Unfortunately, before we could get to the iconic scene where Rita Hayworth's character was introduced, Alex's phone started ringing on the counter. All three of us just sat on the couch and watched it vibrate and light up as the ringing continued. It wasn't until both Gillette and I turned to look at her that Alex finally gave a defeated sigh and answered it.

She stood in the kitchen with her back to us as she talked. I kept my eyes on her, but Gillette had returned to watching the movie and eating, having once again snatched my food while I wasn't looking. I finished off the last gulp of my beer as Alex shut off her phone and made her way back to the couch. Instead of sitting down, she grabbed her jacket and started to slide into it.

"Work?" I asked, knowing it would be the only thing that would get her out at this hour.

"Yeah, there's been another murder. I'm gonna have to miss the movie." She sounded tired and beat down already. But I knew when it came to her work, she wouldn't blow it off.

"Well, that sucks."

"Yeah, well, you're gonna miss the movie, too. I want you to check out the fresh site. And, hopefully, we can find something to ID this killer before it happens again."

"I told you, werewolves aren't identifiable unless they're in their wolf form. As long as they're in human form, there's no real way to track them." I really did not want to get dragged into this, especially not after the horror show I saw this morning. Seeing crime scene photos is one thing, but firsthand is way worse.

"Sounds like you two could use a hand." Gillette peeled himself off the couch and stood. His back made little popping noises as his spine decompressed.

"Any way you can leave your little friend at home, Halson?"

"You're more than welcome to try, but it'll go about as well as it did when you tried to throw him out earlier. Besides, he might actually be useful this time."

"And I'm going to choose to ignore that." Gillette rolled his eyes and shrugged into his own coat.

I sighed. There was clearly no way I was going to get out of this. I picked up my duster from the foot of the stairs and threw it on, sliding the Beretta into my shoulder holster and dumping a dozen or so mags into the coat pockets. I have a sentimental attachment to my 1911. It had been my father's, but for the time being, I would have to switch guns because the Beretta met my needs far better.

"I can't believe you're still wearing that old thing," Gillette said, eyeing my coat. Sure, the old duster was a little beat up and patched up, but it was the heaviest and warmest coat I owned.

"Yeah, so what of it?" I felt the need to defend the old girl's honor.

"It makes you look like some rejected superhero."

"Says the guy who looks like a bad John Constantine cosplay," I shot back. And that's what he looked like. Gillette had put on a white dress shirt over his tank top, making him look more fashion model and less rockstar. With the tan camel coat, he did look like a long-haired version of the guy from the TV show. It was annoying how well he could pull it off.

"Yeah, yeah, yeah. Both of you girls are pretty. Can we go now? I would rather not be at this all night." Alex stood holding the front door, impatient and clearly not up for our fun little double act of chaos and mayhem.

Boy, she was in for a long night.

"So, where are we headed?" I asked as I wrapped a wool scarf around my neck and added leather gloves to keep out the cold.

"Other side of town to a retirement village. Just follow me and try not to get lost." Alex pulled a wool cap over her hair and ears.

We both looked at Gillette, who just stood there in his trench coat and no extra accessories. He probably had magic spells to keep him warm, but the rest of us mortals would have to freeze.

"Okay, let's get this show on the road," I said as we bundled ourselves out into the cold winter's night.

Chapter 5

About an hour later, I staggered out of my car, my cheeks flushed and burning with sweat rolling down my face. The Road Runner's heater hadn't been working until Gillette had put his hand on it, and then it started belching out scorching heat. I had fiddled with the knobs, praying he'd also brought the car's AC back from the dead as well, but no such luck. Turning the heat down did not affect whatever he had done. While I was grateful not to freeze my ass off for an hour, the heater had instead baked me like a potato, forcing me to strip off my gloves and scarf as concessions.

Gillette had also worked his mojo on the radio, causing it to play classic rock, not that I would've minded had the station he'd somehow tuned into not been playing the "summer's hottest hits," leading off with "Hot Blooded" by Foreigner and then rolling commercial free into many more songs with the same theme. I was actually happy when Alex's Lexus had pulled over in front of a duplex, meaning that soon I could get out in the nice, cool night air.

I'm pretty sure steam was coming off my face where the cold air and snow were hitting me. I couldn't even feel it when the sweat, no doubt, froze on my face.

Alex gave me a confused look at my sweaty complexion and mussed hair. But it quickly changed to one that clearly stated, "Do not embarrass me," when I pointed at Gillette, who was taking his staff out of the back of the car, as a way of explanation.

Next to the duplex, there was a small single-story house. It looked well maintained and picturesque, except for the huge hole in the front where the door should've been. It was made worse by the large picture window next to it, also smashed. As we mounted the porch, I could tell from all the glass shards the window had been shattered outwards while the door had been broken inwards.

Just standing on the porch, you could smell it, the overwhelming coppery scent of blood. None of us were in any particular hurry to go inside despite the cold. We just sort of stood around shuffling from foot to foot while cops and CSI guys ran around securing the scene. I couldn't speak for the other two, but I did not need more nightmare fuel.

After about fifteen minutes of standing around in the cold, a technician told Alex the scene was clear and we could go in. Alex and I gave each other apprehensive looks, knowing what we were about to walk into. Gillette just looked bored at having to stand outside. We shook off what little snow had wafted down on us. Gillette was spotless as usual and headed in.

It was a disaster zone. Like the photos of the previous scene, almost everything had been smashed and destroyed as if there had been one hell of a struggle. The room had been decorated simply with muted tones of eggshell and cream. I say *had* because someone or something had repainted it in shades of red. Blood coated the walls and ceiling and soaked into the terrible bargain bin carpet. It had been a stiff, dark gray. Now, it looked black from the blood and squished horribly as we walked around.

"Okay, go ahead and get your Sherlock Holmes on," Alex said. "I really don't want to try to explain why I brought a vampire hunter and a...wizard to an active crime scene. So, tell me what you see."

"Not a damn thing," I answered.

Alex looked miffed at that. She did not like the answer.

"Look, it's all gore and destruction." I flapped my arms in exasperation. I wasn't really sure what else I could say. It looked like the previous crime scenes. Something big and angry had a major tantrum and exploded someone like a water balloon full of red paint.

"Who was the occupant?" asked Gillette, who was standing by a partially demolished mantle, looking at a smashed photograph of some kids smiling.

"Shelly McDallion, an eighty-seven-year-old retired schoolteacher," Alex recited, looking at a note one of the CSIs had handed her. "Just her and her cat, no one else. She was the only one living here for twenty-seven years."

The pieces of shattered furniture I could put together definitely looked like it belonged in a little old lady's home. Something crunched under my boot, and lifting my foot, I found I'd been standing on shards of a teacup. Great. The big bad wolf had torn Grandma to pieces, and I didn't really feel much like Red Riding Hood.

"Hey, Halson, help me move this," Gillette called to me from across the room. He stood next to an up-ended bookshelf that had taken a tumble.

I slogged over and grabbed one end, and he followed suit on the other. Together, we moved it back against the wall, though not in its original position.

"Help me clear out this corner," he added once we'd finished shifting it.

"Why?" I asked, fearing I already knew the answer.

"I'm gonna try a magic spell to help us figure out what happened here."

I sighed warily as he confirmed my fear. I started kicking loose books and knick-knacks out of the way, and as I did, I saw that the corner was rather clean. The blood hadn't soaked into the carpet in the corner, so it was relativity clean despite the debris. As I kicked more things out of the way, Gillette took out a container of Morton's salt and poured it out in the empty space, creating a circle around himself.

"Oh, God, what are you two morons up to now? You're ruining my crime scene. How am I supposed to explain this?" Alex was predictably not happy with Gillette's latest shenanigan, and I was right there with her. I really don't like magic.

"Gillette is gonna try a magic spell to find out what happened."

"Really? Cool."

"Not cool, just stand back and try not to breathe it in." I motioned her back from the circle.

"Why? Is that bad?" she asked, momentarily worried.

"Not sure, but Gillette has been breathing it for years, and he is clearly not right in the head."

Gillette gave me a rude hand signal I chose to believe was just part of his spell.

Once the circle was complete, a perfect white line of salt surrounded him. He tossed me his staff. I caught it clumsily, but managed not to drop it and cock up everything. From the inside of his jacket, he pulled an old, shabby-looking bronze dagger. He ran the blade across his upturned hand, and a line of bright red blood welled up in his palm.

"Well, I guess he *is* human," I muttered out the side of my mouth to Alex.

"Shut up, Halson. This next part is tricky, and I need to concentrate," Gillette said between clenched teeth. Apparently, flaying open your flesh with a dull, rusty knife really hurts. He tipped his hand and spilled a small trickle of blood onto the fresh white salt. As soon as the first few drops hit the circle, there was an audible sound like a static shock popping off, and then the air was full of power.

Think of those electrical substations. If you've ever stood near one when it's going full tilt, you can feel the electricity in the air all around you, causing your tiny hairs to stand on end. It was like that, but this wasn't electrical power. This was *real* power, untainted, unadulterated, pure magical power. It set my teeth on edge, and I could see from the way she squeezed my hand that Alex was feeling it, too.

Gillette took the dagger and held it in front of his face. At the same time, he sat down in the circle, folding his legs and coat under him, careful not to break the circle. He was mumbling something I couldn't make out under his breath. As he chanted, the power in the room grew, crowding everything in it. The pressure grew and grew. You could feel it in the back of your eyes, and it only continued. My head felt like a balloon slowly filled with air until it reached the point where it couldn't take anymore, and then it popped.

The room went all VCR on us. That's the only way I can describe it. The world went all fuzzy and grainy like old film, and there were even scratches and tracking blurs. Then things started moving in reverse as if the world had been set on super-fast rewind. Ghostly versions of Alex, Gillette, and I walked very quickly backward out of the room, and so did the CSIs and other cops. What happened next, I couldn't comprehend, so Alex and I stood there with our mouths hanging open.

After several confusing minutes, the film stopped. We were standing in a warm, slightly grainy version of the living room, but it wasn't wrecked. The ghostly overlay showed the room as it was. The furniture was all back in its rightful places and intact. It looked nice and inviting, the way a grandparent's house should. Sitting in one of the chairs enjoying a nightly cup of tea was a little old white-haired lady. I assumed it was Mrs. Dallion. I noticed as I watched her talk to her cat and stir her cup that there was no sound. It was like watching an old home video on mute. Then something happened, and she looked at the door. She put down her cup and started to stand.

Before she could fully gain her feet, the front door exploded inwards. It wasn't as if something had kicked it in. Whatever hit the door blew it off its hinges and cracked it in half. The splintered pieces pinwheeled across the room and through the far wall. What came through, I can't describe. Mainly because I have no clue what it was. It stood in the hole where the front door had been, and was what I can only describe as absolute nothingness. It was not so much like a shadow, but more like darkness had coalesced itself into an actual entity. It pulled light into itself and emitted a blackness unlike anything I had seen outside of my nightmares.

The little old lady saw it just as we did, but instead of screaming and running for her life, she did something I could never have expected. She changed. When I say she changed, that doesn't do it justice. Movies have it wrong. They show shapeshifting as a slow individual process with different parts growing and changing in a visually horrifying event. The kindly, little old lady didn't do that. She exploded, or to more accurately put, the werewolf tore its way out of her. Her clothing and skin peeled away as a tall, gangly, gray werewolf now stood where she had been.

It was almost seven feet tall and rail thin. You could see its bones through its mangy fur, and its floppy breasts hung nearly to its waist. Another thing they never show in werewolf movies is that they are part human, so they do have secondary sexual characteristics. She snarled, showing a mouth full of blackened gums and jagged, mostly missing teeth.

The shadow that stood in the door showed no signs of fear that I could see. And why would it? The creature clearly had the werewolf by about two or three feet, having to stoop so that it could fit inside the house. I couldn't believe what I was seeing. The two ghostly apparitions were squaring off just feet from us.

It happened in an instant. The werewolf hurled itself at the shadow beast with unbelievable speed. I could barely follow its movements, but the shadow creature seemed to have no problems and swatted it out of the air. It flew back at us, slamming into the wall and knocking over the bookshelf Gillette and I had moved. The shadow beast moved across the room, kicking aside the sofa as if it wasn't there. Even without sound, you could feel the heavy thuds of its footsteps and the explosive cracking of the wood and metal as the couch shattered against the far wall.

The old wolf managed to untangle itself from the debris of the bookshelf and let out a silent roar of pure rage. Its irises clouded over with age and cataracts, but the look in its eye was unmistakable. It was outraged that its lair had been trespassed in by an outsider, and the only reasonable response was to destroy the intruder.

The wolf leaped at the beast again, going for where its throat should have been, but its jaws only found empty air. The shadow beast had caught it in midair and, once more, threw the animal bodily across the room. This time, when the wolf managed to stand, it did so without its left arm. All that remained was a ragged, bloody stump. Its limb had remained in the beast's clutches.

My mind reeled. What kind of monster was strong enough to do that to a werewolf, one of the most physically imposing supernatural creatures, and the shadow beast had dismembered it with hardly any effort?

In its berserker rage, the wolf didn't even seem to register that it had lost a limb. It rushed across the room again, this time hitting the hulking beast low and bowling it over backward. It crashed through the picture window as the werewolf harried at it like a dog with a bone. Shrouded in darkness, it was impossible to tell if it was taking any damage.

Even with the werewolf on top of it, the shadow beast was able to regain its feet before slamming it to the floor. It was the first time either one showed any sense of impact or injury. The wolf lay stunned as the shadow monster grasped it by one of its hind legs and proceeded to bash it about into the ceiling, walls, and floor. Finally, it slammed the wolf to the floor, bloodied and broken. The beast hunched over the fallen form of the wolf and began to savagely rip it apart. It was the single most brutal thing I think I've ever witnessed. Blood and body parts flew everywhere, and the shadow creature finally liberated the old woman's heart from her transformed breast.

I watched in horror as, after it devoured her heart, it raised both arms above its head and brought them down onto the werewolf's head, smashing it like a watermelon at a Gallagher concert. Again, it raised its arms and preceded to smash the rest of the body into a pulpy mess. When there wasn't anything recognizable about the body, the shadow creature stood and shuffled to the door, where it disappeared into the night. The handful of body parts left in its wake slowly shifted back into the withered and broken pieces of the old woman's body. The coroner had picked up the various bits, but the ghostly images created by the spell remained.

While watching the replay of what had happened, I had forgotten Alex had been standing next to me. I was used to seeing scenes of extreme violence left behind by monsters, but Alex had only come face to face with her first supernatural monster and casualty just a few months ago. Even though she was supposed to be head of an entire department that handled the supernatural, she still didn't have the lifetime of coping mechanisms that I did.

She stood there in slack-jawed amazement as if she hadn't just watched a supernatural snuff film. Okay, yeah, seeing what was basically the greatest VR experience of your life, and the idea of how having a magic window in time could change police work would be mind-blowingly amazing to a normal person, I just saw it as more trouble. I'm really too young to be this jaded.

"Holy shit, that was incredible," Alex said when she could finally find her voice.

"Yeah, if you like watching murder porn firsthand," I added sarcastically, massaging my eyes, trying to erase some of the horrors I had just witnessed, thinking maybe I was the one with no coping mechanisms.

"We have got to get one of these for the office. It would make it easier to figure out who was stealing lunches in the break room."

"Or you know you could use it to solve crime."

"Oh, yeah, that, too." She still sounded kind of breathless and stunted.

I guess your first real experience with magic will do that. Granted, her first time was a real live home video, while mine had been a terrifying shitstorm of fire and death. I was getting kind of annoyed that her firsts were all comparatively light and fun when matched up with my firsts.

"Seriously, we need a wizard who can do that on the payroll. Think about how much easier police work would be."

"You can have mine. He doesn't do anything anyway. But those poor guys in *Minority Report* didn't have a much easier time of it."

Alex snorted and rolled her eyes. "You have always got to go and ruin everything, Halson."

I think we were both being glib in the face of such violence as a way to keep from screaming and running from the room. It was one of the things I liked about Alex. She and I had about the same dry, dark sense of humor.

Suddenly, without warning, there was a sensation like when your ears popped to equalize pressure, and the static fuzz of the illusionary film vanished in an instant. I turned to look at the corner where Gillette had set up his spell. He was standing and had run one foot through the salt, breaking the circle and releasing the power in the room. The air was still, and an odd silence filled the room in the absence of magical power. For just a few minutes, the world seemed to hold its breath.

Then Alex broke the moment of peace. "You have got to hook us up with someone who can do that because it would make my job a lot easier."

"No such luck, love. It takes a lot of focus and power to pull that spell off for just a few minutes, much less what I just did. There's not a lot of people with that metaphysical horsepower, and it utterly wipes you out. I will not be moving any more big magic tonight." Gillette reached out to take back his staff.

As I handed it back, I saw a few beads of sweat run down the side of his face, just in front of his ear. I had seen Gillette do some impressive magic in the past, but he never seemed to have exerted himself like this before.

"So, I'm gonna be the one to call attention to the madness we just witnessed? Fine. First off," I ticked off on my fingers as I talked, "what the hell was that thing, and why couldn't we see it? Second, the old lady was the werewolf? And, lastly, what did it do to her heart?"

"Well…" Gillette rubbed the bridge of his nose as he thought. "If I had to guess, it was probably some sort of cloaking or invisibility spell. That's probably how it's been getting around without being seen. Pretty sure someone would've noticed a nine-foot-tall beastie walking down the sidewalk. I mean, this is Philly, not New York."

"Oh, wonderful. Not only can it pound a werewolf, one of the strongest supernatural beasts around, into the ground like a fence post, it freaking knows how to use magic," I exclaimed as sarcastically as possible. This case was rapidly becoming way outside of my weight class.

"Well, that or it was so naturally metaphysically powerful that it caused a distortion in the spell."

"Is that better or worse?" Alex asked. She was more lost than I was since I knew a bit about magic, but she didn't know anything about it at all.

I was just as lost as she was in this case and shrugged.

"Eh." Gillette wiggled his hand in a motion that meant more or less. "That depends on what it is and where or how it draws its powers from, but it looks like it's hunting werewolves."

"Okay, but Halson makes a good point. Mrs. McDallion was a werewolf? I thought our serial killer was a werewolf, and now it turns out that our victims *are* themselves werewolves." Alex bit her lower lip in concentration as she worked at putting the pieces together. "Could it be that our killer is also a werewolf, and it's taking out the competition, like a territorial dispute thing?"

"If you're talking about competing for food and mates like wild animals, no." I tried to explain, "Most supernatural creatures are near or above human levels of intelligence and awareness, especially werewolves, since they spend most of their time in human form. Even on the animal side, they live in a major city, and Philadelphia has a population of over one and a half million people. More than enough prey to support a large pack of werewolves. Just by sheer numbers alone, we should be looking at a much larger population of werewolves than just the handful of victims you have."

"Wait, are you telling me there could be hundreds of werewolves in our city?"

"Yes and no," I continued. "People who are cursed with lycanthropy tend to take steps to remove themselves from society either completely or during the time of the full moon so that they don't hurt other people. Otherwise, every full moon, you would have several massacres on your hands."

"Okay, so they hide themselves and take steps to keep from hurting people." She followed along.

"Yeah, that's how they survive. Otherwise, they end up with mobs waving pitchforks at their doors," Gillette added from his place in front of the mostly demolished mantle. He looked to be in deep thought, which was odd. He usually had a cocky smile and attitude. It was strange to see him pensive. How unfair was it that even brooding made him look like he was posing for a fashion ad? When I concentrated that hard, it just looked like I was severely constipated.

"So, what was up with the heart-eating? At least one victim in every attack has been missing their heart, and I guess we now know where they went." Alex was back into full cop mode, asking questions and taking names.

"It was probably eating the heart to gain its victim's power," Gillette said.

Alex and I both let out audible *ews*.

Gillette smirked. "It's a common practice and belief among primitive cultures that if you eat parts of your enemies, you can gain their power. The heart was said to contain courage and strength. The Māori people of eastern Polynesia believed that if you ate your enemy, you could gain their mana."

"What's mana?" Alex asked, furiously making notes in her notepad.

"Mana is the fuel that magical beings possess, which gives them their magic power. The more mana you have, the bigger and more powerful spells you can throw around. Supernatural creatures are much the same, but they just have a lot more mana than humans."

"So, werewolves have a lot of mana. Does that mean they can use magic?"

"No, not exactly. In creatures like werewolves and vampires, mana is more like a catalyst for their supernatural powers, like healing, shifting, super strength, and speed. Magic is the act of transferring or transforming energy from one thing into another."

"Like in physics with energy and matter," Alex interrupted him, but Gillette just smiled in pride that she was catching on.

"Something like that," he said, picking up where he left off. "But in werewolves, the mana is channeled into their bodies to transform and enhance their abilities. This is done not by the person, but by the spirit of rage they host."

"Spirit of rage?"

"Yeah," I interjected. "Lycanthropy is a sort of preternatural infection, but instead of a disease, it's a bestial spirit of rage that gathers power until something sets it off. Usually, it's the full moon, and then the spirit overpowers the host, forcing them to turn into mindless, hungry beasts."

"Blunt and not entirely correct, as to be expected from our boy. What is the Order teaching these days?"

Gillette's tone was condescending as hell, and I felt like a kid chided by a teacher. What surprised me was an annoyed little part of me who wanted to tear his head off for doing it in front of Alex. I was supposed to be her expert on the things that go bump in the night, and Gillette was making me look like an amateur.

"In the old days, Norsemen would channel animal spirits into their bodies to make them more dangerous in combat. Of course, the most dangerous animal at that time in Scandinavia, as well as most of Europe, was the wolf. They did this through the use of magical amulets."

"What kind of amulets?" Alex furiously scribbled continuously in her notepad.

"Something made out of the pelts of wolves, like belts or cloaks. But the real problems came from blood magic items like pendants or vials containing wolf blood."

"What's the difference?"

"Well, when you use blood magic, it's a lot stronger than a regular spell or enchantment. Where the pelts would wrap a person in the form of a wolf, the blood spells would open the human spirit, not just their body to the transformation. This allowed the vengeful spirits of the slain wolves to sort of possess the person's body, causing them to lose all conscious control of their actions and turning them into nye unstoppable killing machines. Which, as you can guess, was problematic on the battlefield as they would kill both friend and foe. Time and overuse of the amulets lead to the spirits inhabiting the bodies directly instead of the items becoming what's known as a blood curse."

"And this blood curse thing is bad?" Alex asked, looking up from her notes.

"Majorly," I said. "It's the kinds of things you read about in fairytales. The old German ones that usually end with child cannibalism. The curses work within and are passed down through bloodlines."

"They are not necessarily bad," sighed Gillette, and I gave him a hard look, "but, yeah, they are mostly used to do some bad stuff, and it's some of the strongest magic making. It's really hard to break or get rid of."

"So, it can be used for good stuff?"

"Yeah, but it's not common. Theoretically, you can bind spells of protection or good luck to a family tree. But it's a really tricky bit of magic."

"Theoretically?" She resumed jotting down stuff.

I looked over Alex's shoulder at what she was writing. Her handwriting was tiny and nearly perfect, taking up every inch of the paper. I have no clue how she does it. My handwriting looked like the scribbling of a three-year-old with a motor control problem. I disgusted myself with the thought that Gillette's was probably ye ole calligraphy.

"Well, it's that there really are no cases of anyone doing that, plus it's kinda hard to prove someone has been cursed with something like good luck. It's not like they are winning the lottery every time they play. Magic on its own is much more subtle."

"And Gillette is about as unsubtle as you can get," I added.

He gave me another hand signal that I am pretty sure was not part of a magic spell.

"So, how do you lift blood curses?"

"For the person who was cursed? Death usually does that, but if you're talking about removing the curse from the bloodline, there is only one way to do that…" He trailed off and just let the sentence hang in the air.

Alex looked at me and cocked an eyebrow in confusion.

"End the bloodline," I said.

"End the bloodline? You mean—"

"They all have to die," I finished her sentence for her.

We all just stood there awkwardly, letting that dark thought sink in. It was, heavily, like someone had thrown a wet blanket over the already downcast mood.

"But can't a wizard just do some magic and, I dunno, turn it off?" Alex asked, breaking the silence.

"Possibly." Gillette picked up, dismissing the previous train of thought. "Though it depends on the curse, how powerful the wizard is, and how long the curse has had to take hold. To answer your next question, no one can cure something like lycanthropy or vampirism."

Another silence descended on the room and just stood there. Gillette was in deep thought, and Alex was making notes. I shifted my weight from foot to foot and coughed to break the tension.

"So, did anyone else notice that Grandma turned into the Big Bad Wolf, and it's *not* a full moon outside?" I asked.

"Yeah, I thought you told me that werewolves can't shift at will. They only changed during the three nights of the full moon." Alex flipped pages, looking for the notes from our earlier talks.

"They can't, or at least, that's what I'd always learned." I ran my hand through the stubble on my chin. At this rate, by the end of the night, I was gonna have a full-grown beard. I already wanted to go home and crawl back into bed.

"You're right," Gillette agreed. "They can't. Werewolves can only change during the three nights of the full moon. Not a lot of people know that. They think they only turn on the night of the full moon. But the moon waxes and wanes for a total of three nights, allowing them to go on some pretty nasty rampages and rack up some pretty high body counts."

"Maybe she used an amulet?"

"Did you see her use one? Amulets need a spell or enchantment to activate, and even then, they have limits. It's different when the beast spirit takes over. Their power swells and ebbs like the tides during the phases of the moon. During the full moon, the power of the spirit is so great it takes over the person's body."

Gillette squatted on his haunches. This meant he was thinking. I had seen him do it before when trying to figure out something complex. I don't know how he did it because just watching him made my knees ache and pop. Years of injuries had left my body feeling stiff and sore any time I just thought about doing something strenuous.

"Okay, she didn't use an amulet, and it's not the full moon. So how did she change?" Alex asked, and we all just kinda stared at each other. None of us had an answer. This night had given us more questions than answers, and it was just going to get worse. With my track record, by morning, something would've tried to kill me, and given that Gillette was now in the mix, they would probably succeed.

"If you guys can't do anything else, go ahead and clear out so we can wrap this up and get the crime scene cleaners in here."

I could tell this had totally ruined Alex's night and that she was gonna be busy here for a while, then probably be doing paperwork until the late hours of the morning.

I sighed. Date night was over, and I was gonna be stuck with a lunatic wizard, so my night wasn't gonna be much better.

Chapter 6

We left her to do her cop thing and made our way out onto the porch. I flapped my arms a bit to get my circulation going again. The cold night air was starting to sneak through the folds and creases of my duster. When we'd been inside, we had a small measure of protection from the winter night. But there hadn't really been any form of heat, especially since the front door and window had been destroyed. I breathed into my hands to warm them as the cleanup crew began making their way up the walk.

One of them caught my eye. He was short, fairly skinny, and balding with huge Coke bottle glasses. I'd seen him a few times before at other crime scenes, but could never remember his name, and the only reason I recognized him was because I'd nearly stepped on him a time or two before. He never really made much of an impression. Well, I guess that's the hazard of being a nebbish grunt on the bottom of the ladder.

I noticed him this time because he was staring at Gillette and me standing on the porch. I couldn't really blame him as we probably looked ridiculous with our long coats, equally long hair, and Gillette with his many glittering rings and a staff. We definitely couldn't be mistaken for cops. Then I noticed that it wasn't just him. The whole cleaning crew were giving us looks. By this point, I wouldn't have been shocked to learn they knew that seeing me meant it was gonna be a particularly nasty cleanup.

I get blamed for leaving a lot of chaos and destruction in my wake, but most of it's not really my fault. It's mostly the vampire's fault, but they can't take responsibility once they've been rendered to ash. I take it in stride to be part and parcel of the whole vampire hunter thing.

We moved down the steps to allow them to pass, and Gillette grabbed me by the arm and pulled me across the lawn toward the bushes that lined the front pouch. He then pulled me down, so we were now crouched, hidden from the view of anyone inside as well as most of the street. The closest streetlights were out, so this area was shrouded in darkness and deep shadows. If anyone looked out their windows, we would blend in with the bushes.

"So, how badly do you want to help out your bird?" Gillette whispered as we hunkered there in the bushes.

I sighed. This was not going to go anywhere good.

"What do you mean by help? Because the last time you *helped*, you burned a building down," I hissed.

"Oh, come on, that was a small fire at best and, at worst, a good example of why you shouldn't remove asbestos."

"Yeah, who cares if we get lung cancer, so long as a wizard can't burn our homes down?" I said sarcastically, rolling my eyes.

"How can asbestos be bad for you? It has best right there in the name." Gillette gave me his devilish smile.

"Ugh, why can't you just leave well enough alone? We have a free pass to go home and drink beer while ogling Rita Hayworth." It came out whinier than I had intended, but I was done with tonight. I did not want more trouble on my plate.

"Come on, we both know your little copper girlfriend can't handle this. This is out-there crazy shit, even for being on the supernatural side of things. When was the last time either of us was faced with something we had never seen before?"

He had a point. Between the two of us, we were pretty much the first and last word in preternatural expertise.

"Why do I let you talk me into stuff like this?"

"Plus, you're out of beer."

"I hate you." I shook my head. Gillette's grin was so white, I think it was actually lighting up our little patch of shadows.

He raised one hand in front of his face and opened it. When he did, something fell out, and it took me a second to see what it was in the dark. A small sliver chain dangled between his fingers. One end was looped around his wrist, and at the other end dangled a small crystal. It wasn't cleanly cut like the kind to see in those silly occult shops. It was rather rough and a muted purple-ish color.

"This," said Gillette proudly, "is a scrying stone." His smile grew wider. He was clearly pleased about something.

"I really question your taste in jewelry," I said in a flat tone. I hate being out of the loop. I'm not used to being on this side of not knowing things.

"You don't know what a scrying stone is, do you?" His smile faded as he was clearly annoyed with my lack of knowledge on magic crap.

"Yeah, I totally know what scrying stones are. But just to make sure we're both on the same page, why don't you explain it," I said in a poor attempt to bluff.

"Look, if you don't... Ugh, just never mind."

I'm not going to lie. I enjoy frustrating Gillette. I know how petty it is, but I hate how dumb he makes me feel sometimes.

He took a few deep breaths. He was clearly counting to ten in his head. I don't know who came up with that method, but from personal experience, it works really well when dealing with idiots or annoying people like me.

"A scrying stone," Gillette started again, "is a focus, used primarily to find something or someone. It works by attaching something that pertains to what you are looking for and then holding it over a map. Instead of hanging straight down, the pendulum will be pulled in the direction of whatever it is we are looking for."

"Okay, we have the stone, and we can get a map, but the problem with your plan is we have nothing of the killer's to use." The moment I said it, I realized I'd missed something Gillette had seen because his smile returned in full force.

He reached over and parted the bushes so I could see what he wanted me to see. I squinted into the darkness, trying to get my eyes to focus. Then, I saw it. There was a dark puddle on the ground below the bushes. Some leaves and the lattice work that enclosed the area under the porch were splattered darkly with blood.

"Okay, it's blood, but there was blood all over the place in there. It looked like a Jackson Pollock painting if he'd been a serial killer. How do we know this is the killer's blood?"

I started running over the events we'd seen with Gillette's magic VCR spell. The werewolf had slammed the shadow beast through the front window, and for a moment, it had been mostly outside. So, this puddle of blood must have been the result of the creature being hurt when it went through the glass. Gillette had noticed this before I did, and I was kicking myself for it. Gillette noted realization dawn on my face.

"With this, we should be able to track it down." He dipped the crystal into the puddle of blood.

"Great, I think I have a map in the car."

"Nah, I have a better idea. I just need to modify the spell." Gillette cupped the stone in his free hand, closed his eyes, and started muttering a low chant under his breath.

I winced and leaned away from him as the stone began to glow. Don't get me wrong, Gillette is probably one of the best in the world at what he does, but he plays fast and loose a lot of the time, which is not something you want with someone who is essentially handling dynamite.

Nothing blew up, so I breathed easy and opened my eyes.

Gillette had that pleased smile on his face again as the crystal he held up pulsed with a faint, purplish light. What was amazing was it was no longer hanging down. Instead, it was sticking straight out and to the left. As I watched, the crystal seemed to give light tugs to the chain like a dog on a leash. I know I said I don't like magic, but it's always cool to witness.

"Great, can you help me find my keys next time I lose them?" I said.

"Yeah, no. This spell isn't gonna last long. Once the blood dries, it's gonna stop working, so we have to shake a leg now if we plan to find this thing." He stood and brushed the dirt off his knees.

I sighed again, knowing this would bring trouble, and my knees popped so loud as I stood that it sounded like gunshots to me.

Gillette and I got into the Road Runner and headed off in the direction the crystal was pointing.

He and his little magical GPS were the worst navigators in the world. We'd been driving for nearly an hour, constantly having to make U-turns and backtracking. Turns out, the spell, while pretty neat, wasn't the best at giving directions as it pointed directly at whatever it was we were following. However, the good people of the 1700s and 1800s were not nice enough to lay out the city plans in line with the needs of wizards and vampire hunters driving cars. As we moved, the crystal would either point in line with the road or, more often than not, straight into a building.

I had to take turns at the last minute or try to recalculate and maneuver around one-way streets. Most of the time, I would miss a turn and have to illegally turn around in the street, which is not easy in Philadelphia, especially at night. We got lucky with quite a few empty streets. I was glad our direct path hadn't taken us through the city center. We still ended up nearly on the other side of the city. We had crossed Philly's westernmost bits and traveled far enough north that the neighborhoods were getting worse with each block, and I silently prayed we wouldn't end up in really bad parts of northern Philly they call the "Badlands."

I wasn't so much worried about having to deal with gangs, but more I didn't want to have to try to explain it to the cops after Gillette turned them into a greasy spot on the asphalt. We had enough chaos and violence with the bangers and bikers. We didn't need to add wizards to that list. My prayers were answered when, after turning down one street, the crystal whipped around to point in the opposite direction.

"It's back there," yelled Gillette, craning his head to look where it was pointing.

It was so sudden that I ended up jumping the curb and nearly hitting a parked car. I circled the block, and the crystal swung around to remain pointing at it the whole time.

"So, now what?" I asked on our second trip around the block.

"Well, now we get out and walk to narrow it down." Gillette peered out the car's windows, looking at the buildings as if trying to find something to tell him which one. "As we get closer, it should hone in on it."

"You want to walk these streets at night?" This neighborhood wasn't gangland, but it was definitely seedy. I had parked in front of a pawnshop that was closed for the night, and two doors down was a dive bar.

Gillette gave me a look that said I was an idiot.

Okay, he was right. I mean, aside from the Beretta in my shoulder rig, I was wearing a mag pack on the back of my belt that held ten more magazines, as well as several knives, some other weapons, and an assortment of tools of the trade. Next to Gillette, I was probably the most well-armed and dangerous thing on this street, and Gillette was pretty much a nuclear bomb that walked and talked. Even God would've pitied the poor fool who decided their night needed to include mugging us. Only the biggest, nastiest of the supernatural boogities would've stood a chance against the two of us. Unfortunately, we were hunting one of the biggest and nastiest things either of us had ever seen.

We got out of the car and started walking down the street, watching the crystal. It was losing power as it no longer stood straight out as it had during most of the drive. It was starting to droop heavily. We stopped in front of the bar, and it pointed directly at the door for a few seconds before the spell wore off, and it dropped back to dangling from Gillette's hand.

"Why couldn't it have been the pawnshop?" I asked. "Why has it always got to be the worst choice possible?"

"Because life is a series of malicious challenges that serve to slowly beat you down and break you before you die," Gillette answered in an all too chipper tone.

"God, you are just a cheery ray of sunshine," I replied.

"Life is a matter of perspective. You have to look for the positive." He gave me another of those big grins.

"Sounds like self-delusion to me."

"Oh, it is, but self-delusion is the best type of delusion."

"We're just procrastinating from going inside, right? I'm totally okay with that. I'm just making sure we're on the same page."

I sighed. The odds were high that this was gonna get ugly. If the thing was in there, there was a very good chance they were gonna be peeling us off the walls. I would have to change my business cards to read Tobias Halson: Fine Paste.

We took a few more minutes to psych ourselves up before we headed in.

Chapter 7

I will admit, the bar was not what I expected. I was bracing myself to enter a dimly lit, smoke-filled hole in the wall full of bikers and rock-bottom alcoholics. I'm man enough to admit I was wrong, and I should be ashamed for judging others so harshly. The bar was actually kinda nice. I mean, it wasn't a five-star establishment, and it didn't look like it could pass a health inspection with a grade higher than a B, but it wasn't bad. It was the kind of place I could've seen myself drinking if I was a bar person.

The bar itself was shiny and clean with a well-waxed sheen to it. The stools were bolted to the floor, but none looked damaged or off. There is almost always one bad stool at any bar. This one didn't seem to have one. There were also a couple of booths. One did have some visible repair work, but they were both clean. There was even an older couple sitting in one of the booths, though they both looked like they'd seen some hard miles.

In the back was a pool table and a real jukebox. You don't see real jukeboxes anymore, and I was a little tempted to see what their selection was. It had been playing "Separate Ways" by Journey when we came in. How could any bar that's jukebox played Journey be bad?

A group of younger people were in the back shooting pool. Just a couple of guys and a girl. I couldn't make out their ages, but I would have guessed they were in their late teens or early 20s. This made me think of Cassie and Jake. I shuddered to think of those kids one day trying to tackle something like the monster we were hunting.

Gillette and I had come through the door, ready for hell to leather, and we were greeted with the mostly empty and, except for the jukebox, pretty quiet room. In my head, I wanted to think we looked impressive without long coats billowing and hard, intimidating devil-may-care looks on our faces. In reality, we just made a lot of noise and drew attention as we came through the door. At that same moment, the song on the jukebox ended, and the room was flooded with silence as everyone turned to stare at the two idiots.

The girl leaning over the pool table snapped her gum loudly, and one of the boys coughed. It was horribly awkward for everyone. They all quickly returned to their previous activities, forgetting all about us. We both heaved a sigh of relief. It goes to show you should never try to act cool, 'cause you only end up making a fool out of yourself.

Once we had the lay of the land, we saddled up to the bar, still trying to maintain an air of cool. The bar was deserted. When I say deserted, I mean there was no one at the bar, at it, or behind it. It was completely unmanned. The bartender was nowhere to be seen.

"So, do we ring a bell or something?" I asked.

Gillette shrugged, looked around, reached over the bar, and snagged a beer.

"I would put that back unless you want to lose that hand," came a stern voice from the end of the bar.

We turned to look. A woman had come out of a swinging door that had not been visible when we walked in. It probably led to some sort of kitchen or grill. Based on the patrons in the booth, they seemed to serve food.

She was tall, and by tall, I mean taller than me. I am close to six feet, but she was taller than Gillette, meaning she was well over six feet. She was solidly built, but not overweight, implying a mixture of hard labor and good genetics led to a solid physic. It was easy to believe she could follow through on her threat by snapping off Gillette's hand at the wrist.

She was clearly of Native American descent. I mean real, genuine Native American. Her skin was a deep natural bronze, and she had a head of silky raven hair pulled to the side in a ponytail that draped over her shoulder like liquid night.

"You gonna make me?" Gillette said with a playful tone to his voice that he got when he was flirting with women. He flipped off the cap of the bottle with one thumb and took a swig.

"How about I make you pay for it before I throw you out on your ass?" She stone walled his attempts at flirting with her cold look.

He just shot her his hundred-watt smile, and it didn't so much a dent her icy exterior. It was weird to see Gillette strike out with the ladies. I'd never seen this before. When he put effort into it, his model-like good looks and British accent melted the toughest defenses. His laugh alone could drop panties and smoke inhibitions at fifty paces. I'd seen him do it. She was not even registering him on her radar unless it was her ass-kicking radar.

"Hey, we were just in the neighborhood and thought we would stop in for a drink. What have you got on tap?" I tried to derail any potential actions that would get us thrown out. If she was the bartender, I did not want to meet the bouncer.

"Beer," she answered, turning those cold brown eyes on me. I don't know how she made brown eyes colder than the night air outside, but she did. There was a hint of something dangerous in them.

"Cool, what kind?" I asked, trying to maintain my cheery attitude.

She was clearly wary of us. In this neighborhood, we were either very rough customers or idiots. I chose to go with idiots because people are more willing to open up to you and be helpful if they think you're harmless. I gave her a goofy grin to help cement her deeming us idiots.

"Beer," she repeated in the same cold tone.

"Okay, I think we covered that. How about food?" I asked, modifying my tactic to see if I would get a different answer.

She didn't even speak this time. She just let out a huff of displeasure, pulled two laminated menus out from under the bar, and tossed them down in front of us. They slapped and slid a bit on the polished bar. At the top, in bold print, was the word *Mandy's*. I guess this was the name of the bar.

"So, are you Mandy?" I asked her.

"No, I'm Larah."

"So, is Mandy around?" Gillette asked, peering behind the bar as if there was another woman he might be missing.

"There is no Mandy," she replied gruffly.

"Okay, I give up. Why is the bar called Mandy's?" I asked.

"Mandy was the previous owner's old lady. It was just cheaper to keep the name rather than print up new menus," she answered. "Now, order something or get out."

I looked at the menu, and it was pretty plain. Most of it was taken up with beer and liquor brands, but under that, they had burgers, fries, fried pickles, bags of chips, and sodas—your standard bar fare. They also had a special house basket.

"What's the house special basket?" I asked, hoping to get more than a one-word reply this time.

"BBQ," she grunted. "Gonna have to pay before you see any food, especially after what this one pulled." She jabbed a thumb in Gillette's direction.

He gave her a wink and a flirty smile.

"No problem, m'lady." With a flourish, he reached into his coat and pulled out a small black card. It looked like a business card, but it was solid black. It was so black it seemed that light couldn't escape it.

She took it apprehensively, holding it between two fingers. She flipped it over and looked at both sides, then back at Gillette suspiciously. She turned and headed for the cash register as the jukebox began playing "Heat of the Moment," by Asia.

I leaned over and whispered to Gillette. "That card is magic, isn't it?"

He leaned over and whispered back, "Even better, it's Mastercard." He gave me a knowing wink.

There was an audible gasp from Larah as she rang up the card. When she came back and handed it to Gillette, she had a very different look on her face. Instead of cold haughtiness, it was one of shocked disbelief. She said nothing as she headed to the kitchen to get our orders.

I gave Gillette a disbelieving look of my own.

"What can I say?" He smirked. "Women love my huge...bank account."

Did I mention that Gillette was rich? I mean, like Scrooge McDuck rich. Gillette probably swims naked in a vault full of gold coins. I lived off packaged bologna and ramen noodles, and he's up to his eyeballs in expensive cars and beautiful women. At times, I just want to hit him in the face with a brick.

Larah returned with our orders faster than I would've thought. I guess the house special is prepped and ready at all times. She set down two of those red wire baskets fast food joints used to use, lined with napkins and heaped full of BBQ ribs and steak fries. She then plunked down two beers we didn't even order.

"Don't worry, I opened your buddy, Rockefeller here, a tab. Feel free to run it up as high as you want," she said. She wasn't as cold as she had been, now that she knew we weren't the homeless bums we apparently looked like, but she still hadn't warmed up to us completely.

I picked up one of the ribs and gave it a tentative bite. And my mouth was suddenly full of flavor. The tangy sweetness of the sauce mixed perfectly with the tender meat melting off the bone. I couldn't believe these had been made in the bar's kitchen because they had the delightful flavor of having been smoked over some kind of fruitwood. It was heaven. For a moment, I even saw dead relatives and heard choirs of angels.

"Wow, these are amazing ribs," I said, and Larah smiled. It lit up her whole face and made her look much prettier than when she scowled. I looked over at Gillette, and he was already tearing through his third rib.

As we ate, Asia gave way to "Still Loving You" by Scorpions. We sipped beer and ate ribs. I hadn't realized how hungry I was, having not gotten to eat much of my Chinese food, and that had been hours ago. Even the fries were delicious. They were golden, crispy, and just a bit sweet. I dipped them in the leftover sauce from the ribs, scraping up every last drop.

I finished and sat back on my stool, sipping my beer. I would never have guessed that a monster hunt would lead me to the best ribs I've had in years.

Larah stood there, leaning back against the shelves behind the bar. She'd watched us enjoy the food with a smile on her face.

"You two act like you haven't eaten in days." She laughed.

"That's 'cause those were about the best ribs I think I've ever had," said Gillette as he wiped some sauce off his face.

I agreed and followed up by saluting with my beer.

Larah cracked open two more beers for us and one for herself. She pulled up a stool from somewhere behind the bar and joined us.

"So, what brings you two here?" she inquired, taking a pull from her beer.

Gillette and I sat in silence, drinking our beers and thinking just how much to tell her. We had to be careful. If we just jumped in, we could end up causing her to clam up and refuse to tell us anything or think we were nuts. The vast majority of the world ignored the supernatural and pretended it didn't exist because life was just easier that way. The only people who acknowledged it were the ones, for the most part, who didn't have a choice. People like Alex, whose job it was to help, try to maintain that buffer so that others could ignore it.

Gillette solved that problem for me by jumping in himself. "Well, my mate here was showing me out and about the town." He laid his accent on thick. "So, we were out, and we got a wee bit off the path. Feeling a bit peckish, we went looking for a pint and found your pub."

"It's a bar, not a pub," she corrected.

"You have to forgive him. He's foreign and stupid. He doesn't know how we do things here," I explained.

Larah smirked, and Gillette gave me an eye roll.

"Speaking of which, have you noticed anything strange lately?" I asked.

"Strange, like what?" She narrowed her eyes, looking at me hard.

"Just different or out of the ordinary."

"Like a bloody giant shadow monster that hunts were-wolves," Gillette muttered under his breath so she couldn't hear.

I shot him a nasty look to tell him to shut up, and he just wiggled his eyebrows at me.

"Just anything you can think of," I continued, trying to get back on track.

"Nothing really, at least, not off the top of my head." She screwed up her face, thinking. "I mean, fewer customers lately, but you can chalk that one up to the holiday season and the bad weather."

"How about you? Have you felt anything odd or out of place?" Gillette asked. He leaned forward, placing his elbows on the bar so he could study her reactions.

"I know I'm gonna sound a bit crazy, but yeah, things have felt a bit off lately."

"Like how?" I asked.

"Just, I don't know, off. At times, like I'm being watched." She laughed. "I guess I'm just being paranoid." We laughed with her.

"So, what's with all the questions? You two don't look like cops."

She was right. No one would mistake us for cops. I mostly got mistaken for a homeless person, and Gillette always looks like he just stepped off the cover of GQ. To the best of my knowledge, cops couldn't afford his wardrobe.

"You are right, we don't look like cops." Gillette laughed.

"Then what are you?" she asked, narrowing her eyes.

"He's an exterminator." He hooked a finger in my direction.

"Then what does that make you?"

"Charming." He hit her with his killer smile and followed with a flirty wink that once again failed to break through the wall of ice she'd put up between the two of them. I was impressed she wasn't falling to any of his charms. Of course, it didn't hurt that she looked like she could've broken either one of us over her knee like kindling.

We took that as the signal it was time to leave before she saw through us and started asking questions we couldn't or shouldn't answer. It's not like there are any commandments of "thou shall not expose people to the supernatural world." Aside from people not wanting to believe it, you also look kind of crazy when you try to tell people you kill monsters for a living. So, discretion is more about keeping yourself out of the nut house rather than keeping some dark secret, but it does prevent most of the mundane people from being targeted by angry entities wanting revenge for being dragged into the light. This past summer, I had dealt with a vengeful stalker of the mortal variety, and that had nearly been lethal enough on its own.

Chapter 8

We climbed back into my car, Now, with no leads and no new ideas. Gillette's spell had been a bust, but on the positive side, we'd accidentally found the best BBQ ribs in Philly, and possibly my favorite new spot. I made a mental note to talk Alex into trying it out the next time we both had a free night.

"So, what now? I hope you have another idea 'cause I don't," I said to the darkened car interior.

Gillette was uncharacteristically quiet. He was always noisy and making jokes. The only times I had known him to go silent like this was when he was thinking.

"Is there a way to get around the back of the place?" He turned around in his seat to look down the street.

"Hmm, there might be a back alley for trash pickup since it's a place of business," I answered, wondering what he had up his sleeve.

"Great, let's move the car and see what shakes loose."

I raised an eyebrow at this, as once again, Gillette had picked up on something I hadn't. I wracked my brain, trying to think of what it could've been as I crept the car down the dark street. Most of the streetlights didn't seem to be working. Kids had a habit of shooting them out for fun, and the city just got tired of replacing them. I turned the corner and spotted the alley. It was rather wide to accommodate the city's garbage trucks.

The Road Runner was a big, old muscle car, but two of them could have easily sat side by side with room to spare on each side. So, I had no problems slipping the car into the shadow of a nearby dumpster, giving us a good view of what I guessed to be the bar's back door while mostly concealing us from sight without looking like we were hiding. We were just two guys sitting in a car in the dark, like easy targets.

"So, what are we looking for?" I finally asked after sitting in silence for a bit.

"Dunno," was the answer.

I was getting a bit frustrated with Gillette's silent treatment. He'd been pushing my buttons all night, and it was starting to wear thin on my nerves.

"If you don't know what we're looking for, why are we sitting here? What did I miss in there that has us hiding behind a dumpster which, judging by the smell, is full of really bad meat or really good cheese?" I snapped.

Gillette gave me a sideways look and a sly smile that made me want to hit him. "The Bartender."

"Yeah, what about her?"

"She didn't react to my flirting."

"Oh, well, a woman not falling for your charms, that is a clear indicator of evil forces. Why are we just sitting here? Let's charge in and burn the place down." My voice steadily got higher and louder as I put more and more sarcasm into it.

"You've probably figured out that I put a little magic into my flirting. Nothing malicious, just a little glamour illusion," Gillette dryly explained as he chewed absentmindedly on a toothpick that he'd conjured from somewhere.

"That doesn't sound entirely...ethical. In fact, I'm pretty sure it's borderline assault of some kind."

"Put your bleeding heart back in. It's harmless fairy magic." He sighed. "And, the only reason it wouldn't work is if the person is some kind of preternatural being, allowing them to break or see through glamour. So, whoever or whatever she is, she knows her way around magic."

"Okay, so your magic spell led us here, and here just happens to be a bar owned by someone who knows magic. That's a pretty big coincidence..." I trailed off, not liking where this was going.

"You wish it was a coincidence."

"I'm just saying you could be wrong. I mean, you have been wrong before."

"Wizards are never wrong. The universe just disagrees with us sometimes."

"And what if you are?" I asked, on the one hand hoping he was wrong, but on the other that we weren't sitting here like idiots for nothing.

"Well, then I would laugh at the irony," he whispered as he pointed one finger out the windshield.

I followed his finger, and at first, I couldn't see anything, until one of the building's shadows broke away from the depths of the alley and began slowly shuffling its way toward us.

"Damn it, damn it, damn it," I swore as we scrambled out of the Road Runner.

I reached back through the window and flipped on the high beams, catching the creature mid-stride, causing it to freeze in its tracks several yards from the bar's back door and raise one arm to shield itself from the light.

Gillette and I took up positions in front of the car, facing the shadow monster.

"How do we do this? Hit it hard and fast with the nuclear option and pray it goes down for the count?" I drew the Beretta and checked to make sure I had a round chambered.

"Sure, if you want to burn down a whole city block and have to explain it to that pretty blonde cop of yours." Gillette grinned. "No, lad, stand back and let the wizard show you how it's done, 'cause you got to use magic to fight magic." He raised his right hand toward the beast and forked his fingers in a way that had to be very uncomfortable. A bolt of lightning shot out from his long fingers toward his target.

Watching Gillette barbecue things with his favorite lightning spell was always impressive. There was a blinding flash, a clap of thunder, and the lightning snaked down the alley at high speed to turn the shadow monster into a greasy spot, and...he missed. The bolt jigged to the left at the last second and struck a dumpster with a sound like a gong. It hit with so much force the dumpster was thrown into the wall, causing several bricks to crack and bits to fly.

I snickered and turned to give Gillette my own shit-eating grin. "Wanna give that one another shot, oh mighty Gandalf?" I laughed. I know we were facing down something that could kill us in seconds, but I'd never seen Gillette flub up before, and the tension was making me a little hysterical.

"Shut up, yah sausage," he snarled. "It's lighting. It's not like I can direct it. I just point in a direction and unleash it. It still acts and behaves like lightning." He repeated the hand gesture, and another bolt arced with the same result. This time, it jumped up to the right and hit an electrical pole, causing a chain reaction. The transformer exploded in a shower of sparks raining down on the alley.

"Want a mulligan?" I asked.

"Shut it."

Gillette was starting to get a little annoyed. I doubt he was used to his magic being useless. He shifted his weight before raising his right hand again, this time, palm open and, a gout of fire leaped into being. If there's anything Gillette loves as much as throwing electricity, it's wielding fire. Though things tend to catch fire and burn that were not intended to. He did his best impersonation of a human flamethrower, turning the alley into an inferno. Heat washed over me as the wave of fire engulfed the shadow creature in a giant fireball.

After about a couple of minutes in hell's asshole, he started letting up on the fire. As the intensity faded, it became clear it was having no effect. The flames were not acting like they should have. Instead of charring the beast into a blackened briquette, they stopped about a foot or so in front of it and sort of flowered out as if hitting an invisible barrier. Once Gillette ceased his spell, it was obvious the only damage it caused were scorch marks on the asphalt and slagging the poor dumpster he'd brutalized with his first lightning strike.

"Bugger, it's got some sort of protective shield," he hissed through clenched teeth. Sweat was pouring down Gillette's face.

I guess whatever spell he'd done earlier must've really pushed him because it's rare Gillette ever flags. His magic rings house not only different spells, but protect him from them as well. While the alleyway was now an oven, the heat itself shouldn't have affected him at all, so he had to be really exerting himself.

"Let's see how it holds up to something with a little more substance." I was putting on false bravado. I didn't know if bullets would have any more effect than Gillette's magic. There's a huge difference between a small amount of flying lead and the forces of nature. The shadow beast just stood there as if it was confused at the two tiny mortals trying to annoy it with bright lights and loud noises.

I took aim, dead center mass, and fired off three rounds—and I missed. I missed a target roughly the size of a Buick, and it wasn't even moving. It wasn't a total miss. It was more that whatever was protecting it caused the bullets to veer off course. Two bullets went left while the third went right. One embedded itself into the brick wall and the other into the burned-out dumpster. The third bullet that went to the right struck the creature in the middle of its upper arm.

The creature let out a shriek when the bullet hit its arm. I was about to fire again when the shadow creature changed. However, change is not the right word. It was more like whatever magic that was surrounding it dispelled. The darkness that seemed to make up its body parted like ethereal curtains revealing its true face.

It was a walking nightmare. It was some murky, twisted creature that stalks the darkest recesses of human fears. I wished it stayed shrouded in darkness because it didn't just hide what it was, but also its sounds and smells.

It was eight feet tall and looked like a man. By man, I mean it had the chest and torso of a man. From the waist down, it had the body of a deer or moose if it that deer was the equivalent of a Clydesdale. Its legs were heavily muscled and visible through its thick, matted fur. The hooves were roughly the size of hubcaps and looked as if they could easily crush a car flatter than a pancake. Its shoulders and upper arms were lean, strong, human-looking arms, but below the elbow, they became long furry forearms ending in three-finger hands tipped with wicked black claws.

The face was the worst part. It had the head and neck of a deer with the same thick, matted fur. Except the face was just a skull. There was no skin or muscle, just white bone stained with blood, and more blood dripped steadily from its bony jaws. The empty eye sockets were bottomless, soulless black pits. Like fading embers, a red glow burned deep in those cold voids. I had seen eyes like those in my nightmares every night. Its rack of antlers was massive and crusted with mold and moss.

The smell was just as bad. When the barrier was broken, it rolled out and filled the alley with the stench of dank body order, rotten eggs, and that coppery metallic blood scent. It crowded the air. I choked on it and tried my hardest not to throw up. Gillette actually staggered as it nearly bowled him over. I pulled my scarf up over my nose and breathed heavily through my mouth.

The creature opened its maw and let out another screeching wail. Its shrill scream sounded like rusty metal scraping against each other. I had to clap my hands over my ears, or it felt like they would start bleeding. Another gust of foul-smelling breath rolled from its gullet, and flecks of blood sprayed from its jaws. Pure, unadulterated rage emitted from every ounce of the beast as it bellowed. It was as if it was trying to decimate the entire night with its scream of blinding hatred.

The bullet that struck the creature left a small, dark hole in its bicep. Normally, it would've been impossible to make out at that distance, except what looked like fire jetted from the wound. A bright blue flame, like a pilot light, was shooting from the wound. It flickered and gave off light, though if it made a sound, I couldn't hear it. I could hardly be blamed as I was staring in open mouthed horror mixed with mild bewilderment. I had never seen any creature like this, much less one that bled fire. That didn't seem fair.

Neither the bullet wound, nor the flame emitting from it seemed to bother the creature in the slightest. It cocked its long face to look at it, then with the effort it would take me to pop the top off a beer bottle, it tore its arm off at the shoulder. We continued to watch in complete disbelief as it then proceeded to eat its own arm.

Okay, I've seen some crazy stuff in my career fighting vampires. I've seen them lift cars, move faster than the naked eye, and even mess with my mind, but I've never seen them do something even remotely like this. Both of us just watched in silent horror as it casually cannibalized itself. It opened its wide maw, and in seconds, the arm was just gone. It gave a raspy, throaty noise and then made a wet, retching motion. Something flew from its jaws and made a metallic sound as it bounced across the ground. It had not only just torn off and eaten its arm, but spat out the silver bullet that had been embedded in its flesh.

A rattling hiss began issuing from its skull as its hairy shoulders started shaking. From the now-empty socket erupted a shard of glistening white bone. It continued to grow in length as sinew and muscle formed around it and crawled down its length. It continued with the elbow, forearm, and hand. It was mesmerizing to watch as the arm reformed itself. And skin crawled along it, covering the wet muscles and tendons before sprouting thick fur. In less than a minute, the arm had regrown and was as good as new.

No wonder it hadn't rushed at us and ground us into hamburger meat the moment we got out of the car. Things that can regenerate like that don't view mortals like us as threats. In fact, it probably regarded us the same way it did an ant. Tiny and annoying, but no real risk. All it had to do was walk right over and step on us, and there wasn't much we could do to fight back. Even running would be pointless. With its size, it could probably catch us easily. A lot of people have this misconception the bigger a person or animal is, the slower they are. This isn't true, especially for the supernatural.

It made to take a step forward, and on pure reflex, I raised my gun, aiming it at its face, preparing to go down fighting, and it flinched. It didn't just do a little jerk. It raised its arms to protect its face when I'd aimed. I squared my feet, settling into a shooter's stance. I raised the gun again and leveled the sights between its eyes. The beast stepped back as if scared of the gun. It had shrugged off Gillette's major league magic like it was nothing, and I had barely managed to wing it. Had I somehow hurt it more than I thought?

I pulled the trigger, this time emptying the clip at the monster. When the gun ran dry, my hands automatically slapped a fresh mag in and released the slide. But before the magazine even slid home, the beast vanished. It pulled the shadows back around it with another ear-splitting shriek, and in a blur of motion my eyes could barely detect, it barreled back down the alley in the direction it came. It was gone, leaving only its lingering stench on the breath of the wind.

"That did not just happen. Tell me we did not just see that," I stuttered, barely able to keep my hands from shaking from the sudden spike of adrenaline dumped into my body.

Gillette's mouth moved, but I couldn't hear anything. My ears were still ringing from the gunshots. He grabbed my arm and pulled me towards the car until I got the gist of what he was saying. Once back in my car, Gillette rolled down the window and lit a cigarette. He took a long drag and blew the smoke out the window.

I just gripped the steering wheel until my knuckles turned white. I took several deep breaths and tried to come to terms with what had just happened. There was no way we could kill that thing. It was big, strong, fast, and it could use some type of rudimentary magic. It had only had the cloaking and shielding, but what if it could do more? Hell, it didn't need more. With that speed and its ability to hide itself in shadows, it could just run up behind us and crush our skulls like walnuts. I nervously turned to look out the back window to make sure it didn't circle the block to come up behind us.

"Relax," Gillette said. "It's gone. I can feel the magical interference it causes now that I know what I'm looking for."

"What was that thing?" I gasped between deep breaths.

"I have no idea. Never seen one before," he replied thoughtfully as if he was lost in thought.

"Did you see what it did with its arm? It freaking ate its own arm and regrew it!"

"Yeah, I saw, though I'm more concerned with how it was able to negate magic like that. It's not something simple or easy to divert magic like that. Hell, it's not something a mindless monster could do. And what was up with how it reacted to you shooting it?" He turned to look at me.

The lit cigarette glowed in the darkness. Its red cherry reminded me of the creature's eyes, and a shiver ran down my spine. I couldn't help but look over my shoulder again.

"What kind of bullets are you using?" he asked. The shadows in the darkness of the car made him look kind of sinister.

"Homemade silver tips," I answered, cycling the slide to eject a round. I tossed it to him, and he caught it in one deft hand.

He rolled it between his fingers and held it to his eyes to examine it. "Hmm, silver. Yeah, that makes some sense. Several preternatural creatures have reactions to the stuff. So, it seems, does Bambi."

"We are not going after that thing, are we?" I asked. In my mind, I was screaming, *no way in hell.*

"Bugger me, no. We need to regroup and prepare before we hit this thing again."

He flicked the cigarette butt out the window, and I started up the car. I let out a sigh of relief. We'd made it through the night alive.

"Nothing could be worse than this night has been," I said darkly. I was done with tonight. The first thing I was gonna do when I got home was take a hot shower and then pass out in bed.

"How about that?" Gillette asked, pointing through the windshield, and I got a sense of déjà vu.

I let out a sad moan and slowly followed the direction he was pointing.

There was a werewolf standing in front of my car. It wasn't just a werewolf. It was a monster werewolf. I know that sounds redundant, but compared to the little old lady and even to the shadow monster, this thing wasn't just huge—it was massive. It had to be nine or ten feet tall, and its body was a professional bodybuilder's greatest fantasy. Every single muscle stood out in perfect detail. You could see every one of them as they rippled, even under the sleek fur. What really caught my eye was its breasts. They were the size of beach balls. It was all I could do to tear my eyes away from them.

Tonight was becoming a sensory overload for me. I was seeing things I was pretty sure no one was supposed to see. First, there was a fight to the death between monsters, then self-mutilation and cannibalism, and now giant furry knockers. Some days, my life was just too weird to be believable.

It leaned forward over the Road Runner's hood to peer the through the windshield at us. I couldn't help but notice the whole thing looked like some bizarre parody of a hot rod pinup calendar. As the werewolf looked in at us, our gazes met, and I could see not only anger but intelligence in its eyes. It recognized us and let out a deafening roar that drowned out not only the loud noise of the engine and the radio, but even the thoughts in my head.

It reached out with its gigantic fore paws, each the size of a manhole cover, and seized the fenders on each side of the car.

With a mighty heave, it flipped the car. The world became a confusing madness of sights, sounds, and sensations. When I say it flipped the car, I don't mean over on its side or roof. It was so strong it caused the car to do one and a half complete rotations before coming to rest on its roof.

Gillette, who had always flaunted our seatbelt laws, proclaiming his immortality, received a karmic kick in the pants as the force of the roll sucked him out the open window and threw him from the car. I was suffering my own hell as my seatbelt, while keeping me in the car, still allowed me to bounce about the driver's side of the car like a pinball. Just as I suspected, I was reaching the all-time high score when my head struck the window frame with a sickening impact.

Lights exploded behind my eyes as I was plunged into the depths of unconsciousness.

Chapter 9

I t was dark, and a light rain pattered on my head as I crouched in the shadows outside the cave entrance. I'd been tracking the vampire all day. At times, following it from out of sight, while others, casting about and following its tracks and leavings. You couldn't be too careful as their senses were well beyond humans. They can see in the dark and have a sense of smell on par with bloodhounds. I couldn't afford to take risks, but I had to maintain a delicate balance of following outside of its range while not losing its trail. My uncle Dale taught me to track with animals, but a vampire was much smarter and faster than any animal. If I made a mistake, it could turn and kill me before I even knew I screwed up.

For the past two weeks, a vampire had been attacking farmhouses and cabins in the mountains of West Virginia, where I lived with my relatives since my parents' death. The attacks started on the night of a particularly nasty thunderstorm and proceeded to escalate. The families were brutally murdered, and the kids, if any, were never found. Everyone was scared they would be next.

I remember after the third attack my uncle Dale came home very upset. They were convinced this was the work of a vampire called the Storm Rider. An oddity for a vampire, as most stake out territories and set up lairs or nests. He was a transient and traveled extensively throughout the States, never staying in any one place for long. He would arrive in an area and build a spider hole where he would wait for the next big storm.

Under the cover of the storm, he would attack a family home and murder the whole family, save the children. They would be taken back to his hole, where he would keep them for his amusement while awaiting his next kill. They were always found later, full of horrible, depraved acts of torture and death. The Storm Rider wanted the hunters of the Order to know what he had done. This taunting and his luck at keeping one step ahead of them earned him a rather notorious bounty rivaling the likes of Dracula or Camilla.

I'd been training in hunting vampires for nearly four years, and had begged my uncle to take me with him on this hunt. He refused. Not because I was too young, but because I was too eager. He thought my eagerness and lack of experience would lead me to be careless, and be more dangerous to myself and others than the vampire.

It turned out he was right.

While Dale led the Order on their searches for the Storm Rider, I had snuck into his office to look at the photos and reports of the attacks. On the wall, he'd tacked up a map of the county with push pins where the attacks had happened. Each was numbered. I stared at the map for what seemed like hours until I spotted what they'd all missed. The attacks were in a pattern, and I figured out where his next one was going to be.

I raided the gun cabinet, taking with me a shotgun, a belt of ammo, several knives, and father's old Colt 1911. I set off to the house where I believed he would attack next without telling anyone, determined to take the vampire down myself and prove my uncle wrong.

I'd been right, but arrived too late. It had already attacked the house and was inside when I arrived. I waited outside and followed when it left.

Killing it would have doomed the abducted children to a slow death if we couldn't find his lair. In the past, they had only been found when the Storm Rider wanted them found. So, I took it slow, and put forth every ounce of effort into tracking him. Never before had I cared enough to focus one hundred percent of my effort on it.

The cave was little more than a horizontal crack at the base of a sheer cliff. The Storm Rider melted into it like a liquid shadow. I waited until I was sure it was safe to creep closer. The cave was only a couple of feet high, forcing me to crawl forward on my hands and knees. It was a very vulnerable position to be in. I would have almost no chance of defending myself if the vampire came at me in the limited space. The floor was covered in sharp gravel, which made it impossible to be quiet, so I mentally crossed my fingers and hoped the noise didn't carry.

After what felt like a long crawl in near pitch dark, the cave opened up into a small cavity. It was the size of a large closet, with mostly smooth blank walls and no crevices or openings. There was, however, a wooden ladder in the middle that went straight up. I realized I was standing in an old smuggler's tunnel used during prohibition for shiners to sneak out when the cops closed in on them.

After testing the ladder and finding it sturdy, I climbed. The hole must've originally been dug as a well until it broke into the cave as it went up a long way. It must've run up to the top of the mountain. By the time I reached the top, my arms burned, and my breathing was ragged. My guns and equipment felt like lead blocks weighing me down. They hadn't given me much trouble until I started the climb. About halfway up, they felt like they were trying to drag me off the ladder.

At the top was a trap door. I tried to peek between the boards, but couldn't make out anything. Taking a deep breath, I gave it a light push as a test. It lifted slowly and silently. Someone had oiled the hinges recently, so they didn't squeak when I opened it an inch. Peering out, I saw I was underneath a cabin hidden deep in the forest. It had probably been some moonshiner's distillery. Now, it served as a den of evil. It looked to be fairly well maintained.

A large stone fireplace dominated the wall I faced. It was lit, and the roaring fire filled the room with a pleasant warmth compared to the cold night wind or the damp cave below. Concentrating on my hearing, I listened for any and every indication of movement. I could make out someone moving behind me, but from my position, I couldn't see anything. I drew my pistol and slowly pushed the trap door the rest of the way open.

The room was sparse, with only a small couch, an end table, and the fireplace as the only furniture. There were two doors, one which led outside and had been boarded shut. The other probably led to a bedroom or a bathroom. I couldn't tell exactly how big the cabin was. Some hunting cabins were little more than shacks, while some of the vacation ones were quite luxurious. While this didn't seem to be the latter, it was also not the former.

I scanned the room with my gun drawn, and seeing nothing, I made my way out of the hole. Quiet as I could be, I closed the trapdoor.

The second it closed, I was hurtled across the room at incredible speed. My back hit the wall with teeth-rattling force, followed shortly by the rest of me. I slid to the floor like a marionette with its strings cut. My limbs refused to move, and I couldn't tell if it was the shock of the hit, which was why I hadn't registered the pain yet, or because my spine had snapped, paralyzing me.

Five years prior, a vampire had torn my back open. There was now a long, jagged scar where the wound had exposed my naked spine. It had taken two years of rehab and medical care to get me back on my feet, and every day since then, I'd pushed myself to not just recover, but improve and become stronger than I'd been. Now, it looked as if my effort had amounted to pointlessness, as I would probably never be able to move again.

Sudden motion caused nausea to hit me, as the impact must have given me a concussion. I felt my body leave the floor and dangle helplessly, the toes of my sneakers barely scrapping the floor. My head lolled boneless on my neck. A strong, pale hand grasped my chin firmly and turned my head to face a walking nightmare.

The thing holding me was draped in a long, dark trench coat with a deep cowl and nothing else. Its body was thin, pale, and somehow emaciated, yet lean-muscled. The skin was pulled tight against both bone and sinew. The limbs looked like thick cables wound tight to the point just before they snapped. Its naked body was splattered with fresh blood. More, thick and rich, dripped from its chin as it hissed at me. Its fangs shone in the firelight, but what frightened me more than its teeth were its eyes. They were soulless voids with flecks of scarlet light dancing in that darkness. They were the same dark, evil eyes as the shadow beast. Its mouth cracked open, and it spoke in a guttural hiss.

"What a treat to have dropped into my lap," came the raspy voice from deep inside the cloak. An impossibly long tongue, blackened with rot, uncoiled from behind its fangs. "I have already fed well, but luckily for you, my 'other' appetites are endless."

For emphasis, it ran its gross tongue along my neck and up the side of my face. It left a trail of blood, slime, and rot. I'm not sure if the touch of the tongue, the smell of its breath, or the concussion made me want to vomit. I was tossed over the back of the couch. My face landed on the musty cushions. A sharp pain shot through me as my spine was forced to bend. I wasn't paralyzed, after all. The pain must've been so great that, in order to protect me, it had turned off my nerves temporarily. The pain turned into a dull, pounding throb, and my arms and legs tingled with the numbness of a limb that had fallen asleep. With one motion, the vampire tore off my jacket and shirt, exposing my bare, scarred flesh. The remaining rags of it were tossed next to me on the couch.

Hot tears stung my eyes. I was crying, not from the fear and horror of what it was about to do to me, but these were the hot, salty tears of frustration and anger. Hate welled up in my chest, causing my breath to hitch, and angry sobs escaped my throat. I hated that I hadn't been strong enough or smart enough to have seen the vampire coming and done something. Just like when a vampire had killed my family, I was too weak to do anything then, and was still too weak to even defend myself, much less save anyone else.

I was going to suffer a fate worse than death before the monster killed me, and there was nothing I could do about it. I hated that. It was so unfair that humans were so weak and helpless. I hated the monster that was about to violate me. Most of all, I hated myself for being weak. I blamed the loss of my parents, my brother, and my sister, all of it on being too weak to protect myself. How did I ever fool myself into thinking I could ever take on a vampire myself? My uncle had been right. If only I had...

Through the blurriness of my tears, I could see one sharp image. A small jar of liquid I had in my jacket pocket. *Please*, I prayed to any deity that was listening, *just let me reach it and let it work*. I screamed in my head, channeling all of my anger and fear into my numb left hand. I forced my clumsy fingers to work as I reached out and managed to somehow fumble the glass container out of the torn jacket pocket. For one maddening second, it slipped, and I thought I had lost it, but then my fingers closed around it.

Grasping it firmly in my hand, I wrenched my upper body around, ignoring the inferno of pain in my back, and swung the jar at the vampire's head just as it took hold of my pants to tear them off. The glass jar made hard contact with the Storm Rider's eyes and exploded in a shower of water and glass. Glass cut into my hand, but I didn't even feel the pain as my heart leaped in triumph. He shrieked as the holy water began to eat away at his face like acid.

As the vampire clawed at its face, large puss-filled blisters erupted on its skin. While holy water wasn't lethal to vampires, it did hurt like hell and royally messed them up. Hopefully, it would buy me enough time to escape. I tried to bully my stunned legs into motion, but they hadn't caught on to the run-like-hell plan yet.

I ended up stumbling as I pushed off the couch and fell flat on my face, tripped up by my own feet. I landed on something hard and cold. I raised myself to see I was lying on top of the shotgun. I had dropped it when the Storm Rider had thrown me across the room. Lady luck must've smiled on me as it had landed next to the couch. I seized it with both hands and rolled over. I pumped a fresh shell into the chamber as I did and prepared to give the Vampire a twelve-gauge buckshot enema.

That's where my luck ran out. He had recovered faster than I'd thought and was on top of me the second I'd rolled over. I fired, but before the first shot had even gone off, his thin but strong hand wrapped around my forearm and twisted it furiously. The sound of the bone snapping was almost as loud as the report of the shotgun. As the gun fell from my hand, the Storm Rider used my arm to jerk me upright. As he did, I screamed. The pain from my broken arm was temporarily drowned out by the pain of my shoulder dislocating.

His other spidery hand grabbed the left side of my face, the fingers nearly encircling my head. With the force of a car crash, the vampire slammed my head into the cabin wall. The impact knocked a pair of antlers off the opposite wall. The powerful arm then slid my head sideways, grinding along the wall. Hanging pictures bounced off my face, and my nose broke as I hit a shelf that also broke when I smashed through it.

Storm Rider changed direction and drove my head down onto the floor. I didn't feel two of my teeth shatter, but I did feel my jaw fracture. My head was spinning, and pain engulfed my world. Blackness began creeping into the edges of my vision as unconsciousness threatened to drag me down into it, and I wanted anything to escape the pain. As my vision faded, I saw a mouthful of sharp fangs and smelled rotted breath.

Chapter 10

The first thing I did when I regained consciousness was vomit. A massive headache was splitting my skull and did not help me to make sense of the confusing world I found myself in. I wasn't a scared, hurt fourteen-year-old boy at the mercy of a pedophile vampire. I was a hurt nearly thirty-year-old man hanging upside down from my seatbelt after a big-breasted werewolf had just spun my car like a tumble dryer. I was getting screwed both ways now, and it was massively unfair.

From somewhere around the vicinity of my right knee, Blue Oyster Cult was singing about burning out the night. It's good to know the radio still worked.

I fumbled the seatbelt loose and somehow managed not to land in my own puddle of puke. The sudden drop did, however, cause another wave of nausea, and I added another pile of vomit to the ceiling of my poor, overturned car. Once I had my gorge more or less under control, I managed to crawl out the window.

My head was still foggy, and I had a hard time thinking straight. When I finally regained the ability to stand, the world took a merry little spin and flipped, dumping me back on my ass. I fought back another round of vomiting. Pretty sure there was nothing left at this point. My head pounded, and the alleyway swayed back and forth. I was definitely concussed. I'm surprised I don't have brain damage with all the head injuries I've had. I really couldn't rule that out, though. I could be nuts, and all these crazy monsters were just in my mind.

That got me a little worried, and I bullied my brain back into somewhat working order. I had to keep my mind on what I was doing and focus. After several deep, head-between-the-knees breaths, I was able to pull myself to my feet using the car's upturned fender as support. Once I was steady, I looked around and tried to make sense of what I was looking at.

Gillette had somehow managed to survive being thrown from the car and had either landed or crawled a ways down the alley away from the crash. The werewolf must've seen him and gone for the wounded wizard, thinking he was easier prey. This had been a mistake on its part, as Gillette had been able to throw up his magical shield before the beast could attack him. He lay on the ground with one arm thrust above him, surrounding him in a giant pink bubble.

You know that thing Glenda the Good Witch uses to fly around in *The Wizard of Oz*? Yeah, that's exactly what Gillette's magical shield looks like. Funny as it may appear, it's insanely strong. We had once survived a burning building falling on us while inside it. However, there's a drawback to using it. He couldn't move with the shield up, which isn't normally a problem.

The massive werewolf had Gillette pinned and was pounding on the bubble with its fists...and was actually having an effect. Each smite of its fist caused the bubble to give, like when you squeeze a balloon. While the give wasn't much, it was enough, considering the shield wasn't supposed to do that. From what

I understood, it was supposed to be indestructible. However, the hell it was managing to get Gillette's defenses to react didn't inspire my confidence in being able to stop it.

I drew my Beretta and tried to aim at its broad back. My hand was shaking pretty badly, and my concussion was forcing me to experience the world through a filter of nausea and confusion. So, in short, my aim was shot, but I had to do something. I had silver bullets, and Gillette was safe behind his shield. I took another deep breath, aimed, and fired the clip empty.

I missed. Every. Single. Shot. It was the worst shooting of my life. My target was literally the size of the broad side of a barn, and I couldn't hit it. My sad little display did get its attention. The wolf looked over its muscular shoulder and roared.

For the record, my sudden loss of bladder control was due to the severe head injury and several beers I had, not because I was terrified.

It then disregarded me and returned to pummeling Gillette's shield. As I fumbled with my pouch, trying to load a fresh clip, the werewolf reared back its huge right arm. Its bicep flexed to roughly the size of a basketball as it wound up its massive punch. It slammed its fist into the magic barrier with about the same force as a semi-truck doing one hundred miles an hour. The barrier gave, and this time, it kept giving until the beast's arm was buried past its elbow.

There was a loud pop, and the magic barrier snapped back into shape, only this time, it didn't rebuff the werewolf's fist. Instead, it formed around the arm, stopping at the bicep. Everything below the elbow was inside the shield, and it was taking swipes at the wizard with its claws. Gillette pressed himself against the sloped floor of the bubble to try to keep as much space between himself and the razor-sharp claws that were slashing through the air just inches away from his face.

I dropped the new magazine and had to kneel to pick it up. My kneecap hit it on the way down, causing it to skitter away from my hand. I made a lunge for it, going to all fours. I forced my hands to cooperate, managing to slide the magazine into the gun and hit the slide release. Steadying myself with the alley wall this time, I made my way back to my feet. I had no real plan, but I tend to do my best work playing it by ear.

I'm also lucky as hell that, at that moment, my insanely amazing luck kicked in. A silver sedan smashed its way past my flipped car as it tore down the alley. It lost momentum as it bounced off the old muscle car and careened off the opposing wall, but still stuck the werewolf with enough force to send the animal flying. The car came to a dead stop on impact, the front took most of the damage, and it was clearly totaled. My muddled brain reported the car looked familiar.

The driver's door swung open with a grinding noise, and Alex stepped out of the Lexus. She braced herself against the door, using it for cover, and aimed her Glock at the werewolf.

"Philly PD!" she shouted. "Halt and show me your hands, er paws, or whatever." Oh, God, she was trying to do her cop thing on a supernatural creature that had as much respect for the police as it had an understanding of what law enforcement was, which is exactly none.

The werewolf heaved itself up. Even down on all fours, it was bigger than a car. The fur on its neck ruffled, and it let out another of those earth-shaking roars. To her credit, Alex didn't so much as flinch. She took a deep breath and put a round right between its eyes. It wouldn't do much damage being just regular old lead rounds, but it caused the werewolf to rethink its prey, or not, as it stood and turned its back on us.

Alex took the opportunity to fire off five more shots. All five hit it square in its right butt cheek. I had to get her my gun. With its silver bullets, it could do damage, but she was the only one who was in any condition to shoot worth a damn. As I moved towards her, about to call out to her, another part of my brain alerted me to what was about to happen.

The werewolf had turned, not to flee, but to grab hold of the dumpster Gillette had barbecued. Using the weight of its whole body as it spun, it chucked the dumpster at Alex.

Time slowed as I hurled myself at her. I could see the shocked look on her face as she also realized what was happening. I grabbed her jacket with both hands and threw myself backward, dragging her with me. She cleared the door just as the flying dumpster struck the Lexus, filling the air with shattered glass and flying metal shards.

As we hit the ground, I instinctively rolled my body on top to protect her from the debris. We came to a hard stop, and for a minute, I lay there on top of her as glass rained down. The thick canvas of my duster caught and bounced everything harmlessly off of us. Once the things stopped falling, I pushed myself up off her in a sort of push-up.

"Halson, what—"

I interrupted her by puking on her shirt. The effort of saving her life had been too much movement too fast, and my skull felt loose, causing me to throw up yet again directly into her lap.

"Oh, God, how bad are you hurt?" she asked as she tried to sit up.

I shook my head in answer, which was a mistake, and another wave of dizziness rolled over me. I rolled off her and tried not to vomit again.

She opened her mouth to say something, but before she could, a shadow fell across her, and her expression changed from one of concern to one of scared shock.

I turned to see the werewolf standing over us and snarling. It bared its teeth and lunged.

Alex and I were completely defenseless. There was nothing to do but close our eyes and hold each other tight. I held my breath and waited for the fangs to tear me open.

We waited and waited. Nothing happened. There was the sound of slurping and crunching, like when you run the garbage disposal when there is a chicken bone or something in there.

"Alex? Alex Benson, is that you?" came a familiar female voice.

Opening my eyes, I got an eyeful of a naked woman. Larah, the bartender from Mandy's, now stood over us, and she was completely nude.

My life keeps getting weirder.

Chapter 11

I sat at the bar in Mandy's, nursing a beer with one hand and my head with the other. My nausea had subsided, and I could finally manage to stand and walk without throwing up. We'd pulled ourselves together somewhat, and Larah had guided us into the bar through the back door. The bar had been closed for the night, so Alex, Gillette, and I were the only patrons, with Larah working behind the counter. She was wearing only an apron to cover her nakedness, which really didn't seem to bother her. I probably would've cared more if I could've thought more clearly.

I shifted the ice pack on the lump that had formed above my left ear. My head felt like a bunch of monkeys fighting over a bucket of marbles. Other than that, I only had a few light scrapes.

Alex was in pretty much the same boat. She was a little shaken up, but the most damage she'd taken was a tear in her jeans and a scrape on one palm from me pulling her to the ground.

Gillette, on the other hand, was completely unharmed, given he'd been thrown from a car. It seems it had only winded and dazed him a bit, allowing the werewolf to get the jump on him.

"So, how do you and Alex know each other?" I asked as Larah set a basket of fries on the bar in front of us.

"We were roommates for a couple of semesters in college," she answered curtly, retaining her cool demeanor from earlier.

"Go on..." Gillette smirked, hinting at there being more salacious details.

We all turned and gave him hard stares.

"Amazing. He gets the crap beat out of him, and the first thing that comes back online is his libido. Men." Alex sighed and took a swig of her beer.

I leaned close to Gillette so only he could hear. "Is it just me, or are there too many coincidences happening lately?" I whispered.

"Maybe God loves you?" he replied in a hushed tone.

"If there is a God, he's a drunken asshole," I hissed. I couldn't shake the feeling that, somehow, things were going our way too much. Call me a pessimist, but life was never that easy.

"So, who wants to explain whatever the hell that was?" Alex said in the tone of a disapproving parent who caught their kid doing something they weren't supposed to be doing.

Gillette and I told her how we had found the pool of blood and used it to try to follow the shadow monster, only to wind up at the bar. We left out the part about Gillette using magic to seduce women and told her he had a hunch we should stick around. There was a little disagreement about who was the least useful when the shadow monster had arrived.

Alex showed the same shocked disgust and disbelief we did at hearing what it looked like and about how it ate its own arm. She then scoffed at how it seemed like I scared it off, which I could understand. I could barely believe it myself, and I was there.

We then told her about how Larah, in her werewolf form, had shown up and flipped my car. She was pretty much there for the rest.

"So, what was that thing?" Alex asked.

I shrugged. "No clue." I shoved a handful of fries into my mouth. I was starving, having pretty much thrown up everything I'd eaten earlier.

"Wendigo."

My hand stopped halfway to my mouth.

We all looked at Larah, who had spoken in a flat, slightly dark tone.

"What?" Alex sounded just as confused as I was, and she didn't even have a concussion to blame it on.

"The creature you said you saw sounds like a Wendigo," Larah answered. She kept her eyes on the spot of the bar she'd been polishing the whole time Gillette and I told our story. It gleamed and reflected her image in the wood. If she kept at it, she was gonna end up rubbing a hole straight through the bar.

"What the hell is a Wendigo?" Alex asked again.

"A Wendigo is a dark spirit from Algonquian folklore," Gillette answered. "I've never seen one, and I don't know anyone who has, but I've heard of them. Pretty nasty bastards, too."

"Okay. Everyone stop running around in circles," Alex exclaimed. "Look, I know I'm new to all this supernatural shit, but you have got to stop being so vague about everything and let me in on this stuff."

"Alex, it's okay. I have no clue what they're talking about, either," I said. I put a hand on top of hers. I understood how she felt. She was the outsider here. Gillette and I had been part of this world pretty much since birth. It was our heritage. And whatever Larah's story was, she was also clearly a long-time resident of this side of the spooky tracks.

"The Wendigo is a dark spirit caused by the perversion of nature," he explained.

"Great. Supernatural and kinky." Alex rolled her eyes, and her comment made Gillette laugh.

"Not that type of perversion, but I like where your head is at. No, this kind of dark spirit is caused when nature goes against itself and creates an imbalance in the order of the universe." He took another swig of his beer.

"So, how does nature go against itself?"

"In hard times, such as droughts and famines, it's easy for people and animals to become desperate. In that desperation, they may be forced to or justify doing something unthinkable outside of those extreme circumstances," Larah said, finally joining in the conversation. She slung the rag she'd been using over her shoulder. Reaching under the bar, she pulled out a beer and cracked it open for herself before settling back against the shelves behind her to drink it.

Alex and I gave her confused looks. I wasn't that big into philosophy, and I didn't think Alex was, either. Cops like straight answers. And all this pussyfooting around was getting on her nerves. After how stressful this night had been, I couldn't fault her.

We looked at Gillette for an explanation.

"Cannibalism," he added, waggling his eyebrows at us. "It's believed that when one commits a sin against nature like that, it opens up their soul to corruption and possession by dark, twisted spirits. The Wendigo is one such spirit. Generally, they're associated with greed and insanity."

"Once a person commits a taboo, the spirit takes them over and twists their body, mind, and soul." Larah picked up where Gillette left off. "They change into huge beasts whose hunger and anger can never be sated. The more they eat, the more powerful they get and the hungrier they become. They're beasts of pure, ravenous evil."

"How do we kill it?" I asked around another mouthful of fries.

"Well..." She paused, thinking. "There aren't many legends where people killed a Wendigo, but silver is supposed to wound it, and fire, of course. But to be safe, I would say dismembering it, destroying its heart, and then burning everything should do it."

"Congratulations, Halson, we're back in your wheelhouse." Gillette laughed, clapping me on the back.

"Yeah, sounds simple enough. Except you forget that it's super strong, super-fast, and I could barely hit it. We need to figure out some way to deal with its magic first."

"Magic?" Larah asked, clearly interested in our newfound enemy.

"Yeah, it could cloak itself, and when we tried to use magic and bullets against it, it had some sort of shield that diverted them away from its body," I said.

She put one hand over her mouth in consideration. "Wendigos can't use magic the same way mages or shamans can, but they're sometimes called 'those that walk in the wind.' So, that cloak could be what some Native American legends refer to as wind or mist walking. It's something most spirits can do, but as for the shield, I don't know. It could be the Wendigo's own aura. A powerful enough Wendigo could have natural defenses against such things."

"Something bothers me about this, though." Gillette shifted down in the same dark mood that meant he was thinking.

"What?" I asked. I thought I knew what he was about to say, and I didn't like where this was going.

"The Wendigo are pretty mindless creatures. They're only concerned with eating and killing," he added.

"So?" Alex interjected. "That's exactly what it's been doing."

"No, it hasn't."

We all looked at him expectantly, as if he were Sherlock Holmes about to explain a locked door mystery for us.

"If it was just going on a rampage, there would've been more deaths and destruction, but it's been targeting specific people. It's only targeting werewolves."

"Wait, what do you mean, it's only killing werewolves?" Larah asked suddenly.

We hadn't filled her in on the murders.

"It's been killing people whom we either know or suspect were werewolves," Alex explained. "We came from one earlier tonight."

"Who was it?"

"Shelly McDallion."

"Shit," Larah breathed. She took a bottle of scotch from the shelf behind her, poured a shot, and slugged it back.

"I take it you knew her?" Alex questioned. I could see her physically shift into cop mode as she took out her notepad.

"Yeah, she was one of the people I used to give counseling to."

"Counseling?" Alex started scribbling away again.

"Yeah, well, I call it counseling. It's more that I help people who are afflicted with lycanthropy to come to terms with and find ways of dealing with it."

"Because you're a werewolf, too?" Alex asked.

"She isn't a werewolf," interrupted Gillette. "You're something else, aren't you?"

"Yeah, I am." Larah lowered her eyes again as if ashamed. "I'm what's known as a Yee Naaldlooshii."

"What is a Yee Nahglo...whatever?" Alex asked, looking up from her notepad.

"Yee Naaldlooshii, it's a Navajo term that means 'to go on all fours,' also referred to as Skin-walkers. Generally, they're portrayed as evil because they're beings who gain immense magical power through the murder of their families and loved ones," said Gillette, eyeing Larah darkly over his beer.

She dropped her eyes to avoid his gaze, clearly ashamed of the topic at hand. "Yes, the Naaldlooshii are evil, and they gain their dark powers through acts of sin and perversions of nature, but that's not how I came to carry the curse."

The room went silent, and we all kind of shuffled around awkwardly. I hate long, awkward silences, and normally would've made a crude joke to break it. But Quasimodo was still ringing church bells inside my skull, and I was doing my best not to be sick again. I laid my head on the cool wood of the bar to let it soothe my poor, abused brain.

"It's a family curse," she finally said, starting up again, so suddenly I nearly jumped in my seat. "Centuries ago, before the first colonists arrived in the Americas, the Navajo people lived in the areas that are now Arizona and New Mexico, whose deserts are home to many old and ancient beings. One day, a warrior of our tribe returned to the village having mortally wounded a Naaldlooshii."

"Bullshit," called Gillette, causing us to look over at him. "Naaldlooshii are immortal beings. They can't be killed."

"Yes, they can," Larah continued. "Naaldlooshii were once human, and what was once mortal can be made mortal again. It's unknown how he did it, but he did, and the wounded Naaldlooshii swore a curse on the village. When its spirit left its body, it would enter into the dreams of the villagers and drive them mad. It would sour their crops and kill their animals. Its body would rot and pollute the land, making it barren until the last generation of the Navajo people died out. To appease the demon, the medicine woman of the village offered the Naaldlooshii an escape from death, as all immortal beings fear death and will do anything to avoid it. It's the same fear that leads men to seek immortality."

Larah stared pointedly into Gillette's eyes as she spoke. He turned his body away and idly sipped at his beer, trying to act nonchalant.

"She offered up her body to house the Naaldlooshii's spirit so it could escape death. The naaldlooshii agreed, believing it could take over the woman and regain its power. But it was a trap. The medicine woman sealed the monster away inside her. While the Naaldlooshii did not die, it could do nothing but rage in silence from within the woman's body. The seal would not last forever, for when the woman died, the Naaldlooshii's spirit would be released to have its revenge. So, when her daughter was of age, and her powers were strong enough to seal the beast within her, she transferred the evil spirit into her. So, in this way, it would remain sealed away, passed down from mother to daughter throughout the shaman's bloodline."

"So, you're the descendant of the woman and have a demon spirit sealed inside you." Alex was still taking notes. I swear, if we had been in school, I would've pulled her pigtails. Seriously, what kind of person actually takes notes? Granted, I was a terrible student, but that's just not normal.

"How are you able to shapeshift?" Gillette asked. "Surely, that would require the seal to be broken."

This caused Larah's mouth to curve into a sort of sad smile. "The seal was broken a long time ago. At some point, one of my ancestors managed to come to an understanding with it. The Naaldlooshii cannot survive without a host. Its spirit would eventually fade away. By remaining a part of the shaman's bloodline, it lives and feeds on our power, becoming stronger with each generation. With time, it became less of a hostile entity and more of a family guardian. We are no longer tied to the phases of the moon, and have more or less full control over our bestial forms. I have used my experience with the beast to try to help others whose souls also are shared by hostile spirits."

"Well, that's one mystery solved, and it explains why your wolf form is so..." Gillette held his hands up to his chest as if cupping imaginary breasts.

Alex looked puzzled by this, and Larah just rolled her eyes.

"Big, yes. When we change shape, our form is much larger than normal due to all the power that has built up over the years," she added.

"Wait, what am I missing?" Alex asked, still confused.

"Seriously?" I asked, raising my head. "Did you not see her giant wolf tits?"

"No, I was too busy trying to save your ass and dodging flying dumpsters," she snarled.

"How could anyone have missed those? They were huge!" Gillette chimed in. He pronounced 'huge' so that it started with a Y.

"Maybe because I don't think with my penis," Alex fired back.

"Whoa, Halson, I didn't realize you were so progressive. Cheers, mate," he crowed, waggling his eyebrows at me.

"You know what I mean," she huffed.

I was halfway hoping she would start pounding his head on the bar.

Speaking of pounding heads...

"Okay, okay, okay. I'm way too injured to argue. Can we just get back on topic here? Wendigo, hearts, Native American werewolf, blah, blah, blah," I said, trying to head off any more bickering. My head felt like it had developed several seams, and every annoying little thing was causing them to widen. "So, why did you attack us in the alley, anyway?"

"When you were in here, you asked if I noticed anything *different* lately. I didn't say anything then because, you know, outing yourself as a supernatural being isn't something you go around doing to everyone you meet."

"I disagree. I find it really helps to speed things along. But then again, people all think I'm a nutter, so..." Gillette ended his interruption by finishing off his beer.

"Can I kill the wizard?" Larah asked.

"No," said Alex.

"Yes, please," I moaned, putting my head back down on the bar.

"As I was saying." Larah gave Gillette a dirty look as he got off his stool, moseyed over the jukebox, and began flipping through the selection. "Something changed about a month ago. I started having these weird feelings that I was being watched. But even with the Naaldlooshii's power, I couldn't find any reason I would be feeling that way, other than paranoia. Then, I started having trouble controlling the spirit."

"What do you mean, control? I thought it was tame or whatever."

"Not exactly. We live more in...symbiosis, but it's still its own entity. It even has a name, Mai-coh. While I draw on its abilities, it's still self-aware and present. But lately, it's been reacting more on its own, as if it's reacting to something. Some of the people I counseled reported the same thing. At their core, these spirits are still animals and will react the same as any animal."

Alex continued her maddening notetaking. "So, you think it was reacting to the threat of this Wendigo monster?"

"Yeah, which would explain why I couldn't detect it, but Mai-coh was trying to warn me. So, when I felt her react, I thought it was to these two in the alley. I spotted your wizard friend for what he was when he came in and tried to hit on me."

Alex rolled her eyes at this, seemingly none too shocked to learn Gillette was keeping his shenanigans going.

"I figured they were the ones murdering the other lycan-thropes" Larah added.

"And you attacked them, thinking they were the threat, not realizing you'd just missed the Wendigo," Alex finished.

"Pretty much, then you showed up and hit me with your car."

I closed my eyes. While the spinning and nausea had faded, my head was still killing me. The pain had become a dull but persistent throbbing. I wanted nothing more than to go home, crawl into bed, and sleep, nightmares be damned. I could've slept right there on the bar. The overhead fans circulated the wonderfully cool air, which helped to soothe my head. I let the conversation fade away into a mild background drone.

The past couple of days had more than caught up with me. They'd ambushed me and broken both my metaphorical knees with a not so metaphorical baseball bat. The adrenaline had worn off, and now shock and exhaustion were setting in. With any luck, my brain would be too tired to torture me with dreams, and I could just black out for a few hours and sleep like the dead.

Sadly, I had no such luck, as either an earthquake had hit the bar or someone was trying to shake me awake.

Slowly, a voice cut through the din and brought me back to the present.

"Hey, Halson, you alive?"

Alex's voice. Apparently, I had drifted off a bit while they'd been talking.

"Ugh, God, I hope not, 'cause that means whoever is shaking me is gonna have to die a bloody and slow death." I moaned.

"You shouldn't be sleeping with a head injury. Let's get you to a hospital," she said.

"No, no, I'm fine." I groaned. "Nothing is broken. It's just a little bump. I'll be fine."

"You're slurring your speech."

"I'm exhausted. I need to sleep."

"Hey, Gillette, I've got to take care of the mess out back. Then they'll probably need me back at the station to follow up on the last murder scene. Think you can take Halson home and make sure he doesn't stop breathing in his sleep or something?" she said over my head to someone, Gillette, I guess. I was too tired and sore to look.

"I can take him home, but I can't stick around. I'm gonna hit up some of my contacts and see if I can find out what's going on, but I got to do that before the sun rises."

"What happens when the sun comes up?" someone asked.

"I'm going back to my nice penthouse hotel suite and going to bed." Typical Gillette, but after all the magic he'd slung around tonight, I wouldn't have been surprised to learn he was just as wiped out as I was, only better at hiding it.

"You are a piece of work, you know that."

"Even worse, love, I'm a coward." I could almost hear the wink in his voice.

"I'll do it," came a third voice. Larah, I guessed. The fog of pain and exhaustion was rolling over my brain again, making it hard to think.

"I hate to impose," said Alex.

"It's not just that he's injured. You guys managed to wound the Wendigo, and they're rather vengeful. Well, most Native American spirits are, but the Wendigo will hunt down and kill those who it sees as prey or enemies. So, I can watch over him and protect him if the Wendigo shows up again."

"In that case," said Gillette, "I can make a pitstop and ward up Halson's place. It won't last more than a day or two, but it should keep Bambi from kicking in his front door."

"Okay, good. I'll let you two get him out of here before I call this in," said Alex.

Larah and Gillette got me under the shoulders and managed to drag me out of the bar and into an Uber. I made some halfhearted, snide comments about German words, but the rest of the ride was a blur of lights and movement. I laid my head against the cool glass window for only a few seconds before someone dragged me out of the car again.

I must've dozed off because we were outside my building's front gate. The pair helped me stumble to the side door that was used to go in and out. There were a few minutes of confused fumbling for my keys before I remembered they were still in my wrecked car in the alley behind Larah's bar.

This didn't seem like much of a hurdle for Gillette. He pulled his magic wand from his coat pocket, pointed it at the lock, and flicked his wrist. The door popped open.

"Wizards get all the fun toys," I slurred.

"Yeah, we do, it's really unfair." Gillette laughed, getting under my arm again to support me.

We all managed to cross the factory floor, where Gillette used his wand again to unlock the cage door. Once inside, they dropped me none too carefully onto my sofa. Gillette went off to prepare his warding spell, and Larah set about helping me get my boots off and find some pain killers.

"Do you have a medicine cabinet or a first aid kit with aspirin?" she asked.

I pointed past her to the doorway leading from the kitchen area to the back.

"Cabinet. Two doors in the hallway. One on your left is the bathroom. If you go in the one on the right, you're shitting in the closet," I mumbled and gave a delirious little laugh. I was getting punchy from trying to stay awake.

While Larah got the aspirin, I watched Gillette. He had taken a five-pound bag of salt from somewhere and had poured a circle all the way around the cage. He went around a second time with a piece of chalk, scribbling symbols on the ground. On the third time around, he robotically danced around the circle, jerking his arms and chanting while hopping on one foot and shaking his staff. He looked ridiculous.

"Your friend really knows his stuff," came Larah's voice over my shoulder. She'd returned with water and aspirin.

I took both and swallowed the pills as fast as I could. "What do you mean?"

"He's actually working Native American rituals into his ward."

"Why does that matter?"

"It will make it stronger against the Wendigo," she answered.

"So? Magic is magic. What does it matter where it comes from?"

"You don't know much about magic, do you?"

"Not really," I admitted.

"Native American magic is more effective because it was made to deal with Native American needs and problems. You could use European magic to get the same results, but it may require more power or mana."

"Oh, I get it. It's like using a mouse trap instead of a shotgun to kill a mouse." I laid back on the couch and closed my eyes.

"Who uses a shotgun to kill a poor little mouse?"

"Tom and Jerry," I replied, not opening my eyes.

We sat in silence for a few minutes, listening to Gillette huffing and puffing as he finished his final lap of the cage.

"Oi, did you have to make this thing so big?" he called as he bent over to catch his breath.

"This is America, man. We make everything bigger. Our houses, our trucks, and even our Big Macs," I called.

Gillette breathlessly waved a hand dismissively at me. Once he had his breath back, he pulled off the bandage he'd put on his cut palm and squeezed out some blood onto the pure white path of salt. There was that feeling again of the air being charged with electricity for a few seconds, then it died down.

"Now what?" I called to him.

"Now you stay put, so long as nothing breaks the circle, no supernatural forces should be able to cross the ward," he called back.

"What are you gonna do?"

"Head back to my hotel and make some phone calls." Gillette started packing his kit. "If I discover anything, I'll let you know tomorrow."

"All right, man, see you later."

"Oh, and Halson," he called over his shoulder.

"What?"

"Don't die in your sleep. It's a bitch way to go."

"I didn't know you cared."

"I don't."

"I think I'm in danger of working up a tear."

"Shut it." The outside door slammed behind him, and Gillette was gone, leaving me alone with a werewolf.

Larah had taken up residency on my couch after helping me up the stairs to bed. She'd all but stripped me naked before I managed to convince her I was a big boy and well enough to undress myself. She'd taken a blanket and pillow from the downstairs closet and made herself a nest on the couch with the TV on low volume.

She could've played death metal at full volume, and it wouldn't have mattered. The minute my head hit the pillow, I was gone. I plunged headlong into the dark, dreamless sleep of the dead. I was finally at peace for the first time in days. The last couple of days had seen me running myself ragged. Prepping my little show and tell for the kids, then dealing with Alex's police business, and now this whole Wendigo nonsense.

My life had never been easy, but it seemed like lately, it had decided to work me like its own personal heavy bag. In less than a year, I'd lost my office building, two friends, nearly been killed by a stalker, stumbled back-ass-ward into a master vampire's plot, and now a werewolf murder case with a wacky wizard and a super werewolf. Oh, and let's not forget my girlfriend and our ever-straining relationship.

Chapter 12

It took me a few minutes to realize I was awake. The full moon peered at me through the factory's massive skylights. They'd been designed to let in lots of sunlight to cut down on the need for electric light. At night, however, the view of the moonlight was breathtaking. Moonbeams caused the shadows to dance all around me, making it even harder to tell if I was awake or asleep.

Then I caught movement. Something at the foot of my bed shifted. Before I could even think, my hand had found the 1911 that had been somewhere in the bed with me, and it was pointed at the thing that moved in the shadows. Two glowing points of light stared at me out of the darkness. This was the stuff of every kid's nightmare.

The moonlight shifted and revealed Larah crouched on the stairs to my loft bed. Something was wrong, but I couldn't tell what. Something about her was off, and the glowing eyes didn't help.

"Larah...what's wrong?" I tried to keep the fear out of my voice. You never show predators' weaknesses, and that's what she was. She may have been in human form, but inside her was an ancient predator used to hunting and killing weakened prey.

"I don't know." Her voice was deeper and more gravelly. It caused a shiver to run down my spine, but my gun hand remained steady. She shifted her weight, and something about the way she moved wasn't human. It was like she had muscles and joints in places she shouldn't. It was almost liquid-like.

"It's like something is calling to Mai-coh. She wants to come out. She *needs* to come out," she hissed and crawled forward. Her four-legged movement was graceful and natural, all together not bipedal motion. I couldn't help but notice her teeth when they flashed in the light. They had grown longer and pointed. The canines were more pronounced.

I didn't have any trouble dragging my gaze away from her fangs because her eyes were far more terrifying. The pupils had dilated until they both seemed to take up the whole eye, making them look completely black. Unlike the dark, soulless pits of most creatures I encountered, they were not empty. They reflected the moonlight and glowed like fairy lights.

As she moved closer, I could see her better, and it was clear she was bigger. She'd been big for a woman before, but this was different. There was more bulk to her, and her muscles seemed to strain at her skin as if trying to tear their way out. With each panting breath she took, her chest expanded outwards beyond what it should've been capable of.

"C-can't control...it," she growled. "Need to...distract it. Need food or sex." Every syllable was an effort from her as she fought to keep it at bay. Her eyes looked at me hungrily as the beast inside her set its sights on me.

"I will shoot you," I said, trying my best to sound calm, but in a motion I couldn't even see, her hand lashed out, knocking the gun from my hand and sending it over the rail to the room below. My arm went numb clear up to my elbow, not that it mattered, as I had no other weapons close at hand. I was totally at her mercy.

As she straddled my prone body, she tore off the remains of her clothing, revealing a very attractive and athletic body despite being in mid-transformation. Every lean, hard muscle stood out against her skin as she writhed sensually. This allowed my suppressed libido to sneak up and sucker punch terror in the back of its stupid head.

My lower body reported that it was more than fine with being pinned beneath the she-beast. Which was made even more clear when she tore my boxers off my hips with one quick jerk. Her nails had turned black and pointed as they morphed further into bestial claws.

She leaned down and did something with her tongue that caused my brain to stop working. Her tongue was long, flat, rough, and strong, but at the same time, very pleasant. I could feel her pointed teeth scratch my skin here and there, but between the concussion and my traitorous sex drive, I could barely talk, much less protest.

At the same time, some part of my brain was aware of what was going on. As Larah lifted her head, I was acutely aware of the fact she was now at least twice her size. She must have weighed several hundred pounds of muscle and bone, which I could hear shifting and changing under her skin. Her skin was covered in a light, soft, fur-like peach fuzz.

She took my hands and placed them on her rapidly growing breasts. They were the size of cantaloupes and firm, yet soft. They quickly outgrew my hands as they swelled to the size of basketballs. As they continued to increase in size, they also grew heavier. As I massaged them, Larah's growls softened and became more like the purr of a large cat.

It wasn't long before I had the fully transformed super-were-wolf on top of me. Her giant frame eclipsed the moon, which in turn silhouetted her form. There was something eerily feminine and ethereally beautiful about her sheer size and power. I know, I've got to stop taking blows to the head, or this brain damage is clearly gonna be permanent.

There was that kind of primal aesthetic in her lupine form that appealed to our animal side the same way primitive art does. She was a force of pure nature and unfettered female power. Both were beautiful and terrifying. All I knew was my southern region was not complaining. It was more than happy with the situation.

Pinning me down with her sheer size and weight, there was nothing I could do. If I had been rational enough to think straight, I would have to say this position was preferable to being torn apart and eaten. She shifted her hips and, oh boy...

Every movement and sensation was a bolt of lightning straight through my raw, exposed nerves. As quickly as it had begun, I was spent. Though I was breathing hard and done, Larah/Mai-coh was clearly not satisfied. She let out a monstrous roar before her hips began assaulting me like a battering ram. This sent further bolts of lightning through my fried brain. Each movement was mind-blowing ecstasy and delicious agony.

It was as though my libido had set up a grudge match between pain and pleasure, and my skull was Madison Square Garden. I lost all track of time as my body thrashed beyond my control. Everything was pure sensation. I was aware of only abstract things, motions, scents, and textures. Like being in a car crash, my perceptions were fragmented and convoluted.

I don't know how long it was before I lost consciousness. But at some point, I was aware of a naked and sweaty but human Larah collapsing next to me in a tangle of torn clothing and bed sheets.

I sank into blissful empty darkness and did not dream.

Chapter 13

I woke slowly to the feeling of warm sunlight on my skin. My hips were sore, and the rest of my body felt like one big bruise. Aside from that, I felt better than I had last night. My head was roughly normal. The events of last night came flooding back, and I looked around for Larah, but I was in bed alone. I managed to stagger to my feet and wrap a torn bed sheet around my waist.

As I made my way down the stairs, I looked for my pants and couldn't find a single piece of clothing. That was very unlike me, as I usually left a trail of discarded clothing either leading to the stairs or on them. I really wasn't the laundry basket kind of guy, and much of my clothing got worn for several days in a row. Not even a stray sock. Someone had to have gathered them up since last night, and I had a feeling I knew who that was.

I found Larah sitting on the counter in my kitchen drinking coffee. She wore one of my white button-up shirts. While it fit loose on me, it barely fit her. When I wore it, I looked like a scarecrow. She looked like a five-pound sausage stuffed in a two-pound wrapper. It clung to her waist while forcing her large breasts out as if they were in danger of popping the buttons. It was very sexy looking, and my lower region gave a twinge.

Damn it, I thought, *didn't you get into enough trouble last night?*

Needing to put off the awkward talk that was coming as long as possible, I headed to the hall closet. I scrounged up a clean pair of jeans and slipped a mostly clean t-shirt over my head. Now, somewhat dressed, I needed coffee, but that would mean going to the kitchen. My empty stomach protested as avoiding Larah meant not going into the kitchen where the food lived.

I sighed and returned to the living room and picked up the 1911 that had landed on the couch from its tumble last night. I checked the safety and tucked it into the front of my pants as I entered the kitchen.

"Afraid I will jump your bones again?" Larah asked, eyeing the gun.

I made a noncommittal grunt as I made my way over to the coffee pot. I poured myself a mug in silence and took a sip. It was...good. Jesus, was I the only one who couldn't make coffee? Normally, it tasted stale, gritty, and a little weak, but this was rich and strong enough to take the bark off a tree. I'd always assumed it was my secondhand coffee pot, but Gillette and Larah used it to make some of the best coffee I'd ever had in my own kitchen.

That thought darkened my mood as I dug around in my refrigerator, looking for food. I came up with a lone egg, some bacon fat, and the leftover Chinese food from last night. I put a cast iron skillet onto the stove and tossed in the bacon fat. Once it was sizzling hot, I added the egg and noodles to the greasy mess.

When I took it off the stove, Larah turned her nose up at it. "Tell me you're not going to eat that."

I set the pan on the counter, fished out a mostly intact fork from one of the drawers, and dug in.

"It's actually great for hangovers," I said with a mouthful of noodles and egg. It needed salt, so I heavily salted it and took another bite. Once the protein and carbs hit my system, I would be more or less back to normal and ready to handle a new day of potential horrors. I wonder how people who don't fight the forces of darkness start their days.

"About last night," she tried again. "I'm sorry I didn't really have control. I don't know what happened, but it's never been that bad before."

"It's okay," I said through a mouthful of food. "At least you didn't eat me. I'm not gonna turn furry next full moon, am I?" I ran a finger along one of the angry red scratch marks on my chest.

She laughed. "No. Naaldlooshii are not like lycanthropes. It's not contagious."

"Good to know."

"She likes you, by the way."

"Who?" I was confused for a moment about who we were talking about.

"Mai-coh. You're the first guy who's been able to keep up with us. She likes the way you smell," she said, leaning in close and taking a deep sniff along my neck just below my left ear.

"Smell?"

"Yeah. You smell like anger, rage, blood, and death. You smell like danger, and she likes that."

Great, I was apparently catnip for ancient evil spirits.

"Oh, well, um, thanks, I guess. I mean, I didn't really imagine losing my virginity to a werewolf."

"Oh, my God! You're a virgin?" she exclaimed with a thick, rich laugh.

"I *was* a virgin. The keyword here is *was*."

"Wow, I thought you and Alex were, you know, together," she replied sheepishly, clearly embarrassed she had intruded upon such a personal subject.

"We are. I mean, we haven't done anything, but we're in some kind of relationship."

"Sorry if this is kind of personal," she apologized.

"It's not that. It's just we both had baggage to deal with, so we've been playing it safe. Plus, with work and all, it's been merry hell to really find time to ourselves."

"That's understandable, especially early into a relationship. You need your space while you make room for each other in your lives. I was going to say, from what I remember of her in college, Alex used to be very sexual."

I blanched at that idea.

"I do not want to hear about all the guys my girlfriend used to have sex with," I said, trying not to let myself feel insecure.

"Well, guys were never really her type back then." Larah poured herself another cup of coffee.

I shuttered again, and then something hit me.

"Wait, what do you mean they weren't her type?"

As an answer, Larah just gave me a wink and hiked her breasts up. I nearly choked on my own tongue and turned bright red.

"You *cannot* tell Gillette," I choked out as Larah laughed at my flustered reaction.

"Don't worry, I didn't plan to. But speaking of the wizard, what's his story?" she asked over the rim of her cup.

"Not much to tell. Gillette blows into town every now and then, raises all kinds of hell, and then vanishes off the face of the Earth. Like a hurricane, but more annoying and British."

"That's it?"

"Yup, that's it. You know as much as I do." I tossed the now-empty skillet into the sink.

"Do you think he will actually find anything?" She added her empty cup to the sink and turned on the water.

"Despite how he acts, Gillette is the real deal and knows his stuff. So, if he says he can do something, I tend to believe him." I squirted some soap into the filling sink. I grabbed the chain mail scrubber and started cleaning the skillet.

We just stood in the kitchen in silence as I did the dishes. I'm not really used to having house guests, or people around in general, actually. So, this kind of casual social interaction was foreign to me.

Gillette and I got along due to our mutual insanity. We just fed off each other and had a lot of interests in common. Alex and I worked because we understood one another professionally, and our personal interactions were mostly limited to hanging out and sharing meals and movies. I didn't know Larah from Adam. Besides being a werewolf, owning a bar, and making mean BBQ, I didn't really know anything else about her.

This weighed heavily on me, considering we had been...inti mate. I'm not saying you can only have sex with people you love or whatever, and I don't protest it on religious grounds. I just think you should know the person for longer than a few hours and not be under threat of being eaten. I also felt guilty because while Alex and I had never done the deed, and our relationship wasn't exactly defined, it still felt like I had betrayed her in some way.

Larah hadn't done it on purpose. She'd done everything she could to control it. She was as much of a victim of it as I was. I couldn't help but think how unfair it was that these monsters could destroy innocent people's lives with no consequences. Someone had to make them pay, and I guess that's exactly why the Order had been founded. To try to protect people and mete out justice for the ones we couldn't.

Even the murdered werewolves were just innocent people afflicted with a curse. They couldn't control the monsters inside them and did their best not to hurt others. They didn't deserve to die like that. To be ripped apart and eaten by a bigger, meaner monster.

My anger started to resurface, and I wanted nothing more than to tear that Wendigo apart and make it pay for all the horrible things it had done. Those people had families and loved ones who would either miss them or were killed just because they were in the way. My mind flashed back to the pictures of the mutilated kids, and angry tears started to well up in my eyes.

I wiped them away and tried to play it off as soap in my eye. I don't really think Larah noticed. She was in her own awkward melancholy. I briefly wondered if she was also thinking about last night and feeling guilty about it. I told her she could help herself to any clothes in the closet she needed. She thanked me and rummaged around for clean clothes while I finished washing the dishes.

She ended up managing to find a pair of jeans and a tank top while wearing the button-up shirt over it like a jacket. You know, it's really unfair that other people look fashionable in your clothing while it makes you look like a homeless person. I definitely need a new wardrobe, a better diet, and job...and a whole new life.

The rest of the day was spent in awkward silence while waiting for word from Alex or Gillette. We sat on the couch watching terrible daytime TV shows, neither of us trying to make any effort at conversion. Probably out of fear of saying or doing something that would make this even more unbearably awkward.

Chapter 14

By the time the sun started to set, I was checking my phone every few minutes, hoping for a text from Alex. I didn't even know if Gillette had a phone, much less my number, so I couldn't really call him. Thankfully, just before I'd reached the point of pacing my living room, the outside door banged open, and Alex trudged in, stamping fresh snow off her boots, followed by Gillette.

I was actually relieved to see them. I'd begun to worry something had happened. It was unlike Alex to not call or text. I'm still not the biggest fan of cell phones, but when you're being hunted by a supernatural cannibal, it's nice to have the emergency line of communication.

"Where have you guys been?" It came out a bit harsher than I'd meant, as I was still a little miffed over the lack of communication. But my anxiety was quickly replaced with hunger when Alex deposited two large pizza boxes on my counter. I hadn't eaten since I'd gotten up, and I wasn't sure if Larah had eaten anything at all. Unfortunately, my cupboards were routinely bare, a concession to my spartan lifestyle.

"I've been sorting out the mess you three left at the bar, and then was buried in paperwork from the murder scene." Alex was clearly in a mood herself. She looked like a mad woman. Her hair stood up in the back, and her clothes were the same ones she'd been wearing yesterday, only a lot more wrinkled.

"Still would have appreciated a call or something." That was a bit testier than I'd intended. Everyone was clearly on edge, and being angry about it probably wasn't helping. There was also the whole Larah thing last night hanging over my head, and I wasn't really sure how or when to bring that up.

"Well, my phone was in my car when I rammed a giant werewolf with it. It was totaled, by the way. The car and my phone." She didn't sound angry, just tired.

I wondered if she'd gotten any sleep at all as I fetched paper plates from the kitchen. When I returned, Gillette had taken my spot on the couch, the pizza boxes open and spread out on the coffee table in front of them, along with several beers and cans of soda that had appeared out of nowhere.

I sat down on top of Gillette, causing the two of us to tussle for the seat on the couch. He eventually shunted over, and our little macho shoving match devolved into shin-kicking. Alex drug an overstuffed armchair over to the table so she could sit across from the three of us on the couch. I didn't realize how small it was due to never having three people sitting on it at once. Of course, I'd never really had that many house guests before. I'm not really the house guest type.

It, of course, didn't help that Gillette and Larah were the ones on the larger end of the scale and took up more space than someone like Alex, and I found myself crammed into the corner. By the time we had all settled in, Larah was already on her third slice, Gillette on his second beer, and Alex looked like she was asleep sitting in her chair.

"So, where are we now?" I asked.

"Well, it wasn't easy, but I managed to sweep the alley attack under the rug for the time being," Alex responded, but her eyes didn't open as she raised a beer to her lips. "Still not sure how I'm gonna explain several dozen bullet casings, fire damage, and an exploded electrical transformer. Probably blame it on gang kids."

Gillette and I purposely didn't look at Alex while trying not to make it obvious we were avoiding looking at her. We'd not heard the last of that series of poor choices.

"How about your end, Gillette?" I asked, shifting the conversation.

"Well, my contacts—" he started.

"You have contacts?" Larah snorted.

"I have the internet," Gillette replied. "And our guess was correct. Bambi is a Wendigo and a pretty nasty one at that. It seems it made its way down here from Canada over the last couple of months. It left a nice little rampage that was easy to backtrack." He paused and took another bite of pizza. "Unfortunately, that is the end of the good news. Everything else is bad."

"How bad?" I asked. When you tend to live on the darker side of things, you measure your bad news differently than normal people. For regular people, a flat tire is bad news, missing a bus is bad news, and the coffee shop running out of decaf is bad news. For people like me, bad news usually includes death and dismemberment. And for someone like Gillette, it's usually end-of-the-world stuff.

"Pretty bad. Remember how ole double-ugly seemed way more powerful than it should've been? Well, that's 'cause he is. Wendigoag, which is the plural, by the way, increases in size and power when they eat. It's part of the curse. Their size and power increase to keep them ravenous. And this guy has been downing some major league nutrition."

"Werewolf hearts?" Alex interjected.

"Bingo, and that's a really bad thing," he continued. "Normally, they just eat people and animals, so their boosts are small in comparison, but the amount of power in a werewolf's heart is hundreds of times beyond eating a person or two. With each heart, it only grows stronger and stronger, gathering major league magical power."

"Why is it gathering power?" I asked around my own mouthful of pizza. I seemed to be constantly hungry lately, maybe something to do with the cold weather or the impending doom.

"It's not," Larah finally joined in. "Wendigo are single-minded and simply driven by primal urges. This sounds like someone else is using it to collect power."

"Right again. Someone summoned the Wendigo, causing it to leave its natural territory and come to Philadelphia, where it began harvesting magical energy."

We all eyed Gillette, waiting for the other shoe to drop and for him to get to the point.

"The Wendigo is serving as a vessel to gather and contain it for the summoner. As it gained power, its own abilities were boosted and made stronger. This is how it was able to find and draw out the werewolves, and it had to kill them in wolf form to absorb the spirit's full power. One of the Wendigo's abilities is to mimic voices and animal calls to draw out its prey. After it ate its first few hearts, its power got so strong it could metaphysically call out the beast spirits directly. That's how it was able to kill them on nights when the moon wasn't full. It could call the spirit out and force the werewolf to change."

"So, that is why Mai-coh has been acting out of control lately."

"Yeah, the Naaldlooshii was probably responding to the Wendigo's call. Luckily for us, it didn't get to you. That thing is ungodly strong just from eating regular werewolf hearts. If it eats the heart of a powerful skin-walker, it could become unstoppable ..."

He let the thought trail off, and silence fell on the room as we all picked up on the unsaid sentiment. The Wendigo hadn't even really tried to attack us. If it was as powerful as Gillette was saying, it could have swatted us like flies.

"So, why is this summoner person trying to gather all this power?" Alex asked. She looked like she was melting from exhaustion. If she slumped any lower in the chair, she would have been lying on the floor.

"Well, whoever this person is, he isn't a wizard." Gillette leaned forward, resting his chin on his laced fingers.

"What do you mean, not a wizard? You just said—"

"I said summoner, not wizard," Gillette cut Alex off. "A wizard wouldn't need a vessel to harvest and concentrate magic like that. We have our own, and the other was to magnify that power to pull off the big spells. Plus, among the major-league spell slingers, it's seen as a faux pas. It's like admitting you aren't good enough to do it yourself. Wizards have large egos."

"No shit." That earned me a look from Gillette.

"Egos aside, whoever this is has to do it this way because they either don't have enough or any magical power of their own. "

"How much magical power are we talking about here?" Alex asked.

"Well, judging by the number of victims we know of and how supercharged its abilities are, we're talking the metaphysical equivalent of a nuclear bomb."

That caused Alex to sit up so fast, she actually fell out of her chair. "You're telling me there is a magical bomb, just walking around, that can wipe out the entire city," she cried in exasperation. She started pacing the room with both hands stuck in her hair as if trying to pull it out.

"Relax, it's not that bad. Okay, well, it is, but you don't have to worry about it blowing up the city. I don't think," he added, trying to calm her down. Unfortunately, when she got like this, there was no calming her down. This was Alex in as close to full panic mode as I'd ever seen her.

"Okay, so what do they need that much power for? What kind of spell needs magical nuke-level batteries?" I asked, trying to steer the conversation into relativity neutral waters.

"Well, not city destruction, but I could achieve that with far less magic. Not that I would." Gillette picked up as Alex continued to pace. "And I doubt it's a summoning spell. It's way too much magic for your run-of-the-mill nasties, even some of the bigger ones. The only thing bigger would be an elder being from beyond the veils of time and space, and that would require a lot more magic, like a couple of dozen super Wendigos."

"So, then what?" Alex demanded.

"Well, what else do criminals do with explosives when not trying to destroy cities?" he asked coyly.

"Break open bank vaults?" I asked.

"No, not a robbery, a prison break," said Larah in a hushed tone.

"Again, you win the prize. The best guess is that whoever is behind the Wendigo is using it to bust open a sealing spell of some sort." Gillette tipped Larah a wink as the rest of us just sat back, stunned.

This news was just too big. In the course of a few days, I'd gone from boring training of rookies to serial murder to monster horror flick and now to wizard's version of *Ocean's Eleven*. How the hell did I keep stumbling into this crap? Life hates me.

"Okay, how do you break a sealing spell?" I asked. It was either gonna be me or Alex, and she was already having a tough day.

"There are different ways. The easiest would be to know the unsealing spell. But for argument's sake, let's say you lost the key. Well, then you would be left with a few options, like counterspells, waiting for the seal to wear off, etcetera. Things of that nature."

"Or you can force your way in with enough power, like blowing a bank vault," Alex added, taking her seat again.

"Not exactly. Sealing spells are meant to keep something in, so they have to be strong enough to both keep that power in and hold up to raw power attacks. The trick is to cause it to short out like an electrical system. Run too much power through a grid, the circuit blows out, and everything shuts down."

"So, how do you do that with magic?"

"With a ritual, and not a very nice one," Larah interrupted again. "It's a sacrificial ritual where the vessel is destroyed, causing a massive release of power. Done in a place of power like a temple or holy place, and the priest could channel it into a number of powerful spells. However, if performed in conjunction with a sealing spell, it would strengthen the seal."

"Unless...you put too much power into it...and it shorts ou t...turning off the seal." Alex slowly worked out the thread of what they were implying, which was faster than I was getting it. This was sounding more and more like we were out of our depth.

"Any idea on what this seal is protecting?"

"Or imprisoning? No, I got no clue. None of my mates could ferret out anything like that around here. At least, not something that needs that kinda power." Gillette threw his head back and slumped lower on the couch, eyes closed in exhaustion and frustration. It was a perfect metaphor for how we all felt. We were out of our depths and up to our ears in a mess. We had no idea how big it was.

We sat in silence, just letting the gravity of the situation settle on us like a heavy blanket. It was suffocating and maddening at the same time. In books and movies, this was when the heroes would come up with a clever plan, or the cavalry would arrive at just the right moment to give them what they needed to save the day. Unfortunately for us, life was not nearly that fair. Once it's got you on the ground, it just keeps kicking.

"So, we don't know who this summoner is, what they are looking for, where it is, or how to stop it. What we do know is that it's got a turbo-charged mythical bouncer that purées werewolves and already proved it could kick our asses without actually trying to kick our asses. Oh, how could this possibly get any worse." And that was when my big mouth temped the petty gods of irony, and they decided to bitch slap us all with a heaping helping of being royally screwed. I hadn't noticed, but as we'd sat talking, night had fallen, which was when the legion of Nosferatu smashed through the factory skylights.

Glass rained down in a hailstorm of beautiful but incredibly sharp death. Most of the larger pieces above us hit the roof of the cage and broke into smaller chunks, but still, a shard the size of a butcher knife slammed, point down, into the top of the coffee table, spearing a slice of pizza, pinning it and the box to the table.

Alex dove under the coffee table as Gillette brought up his magical shield. Larah, Gillette, and I were safe inside his big pink bubble. Alex hunkered under the table while shards of glass exploded and bounced all around us.

Gillette dropped the shield as soon as the falling debris ceased, and I launched myself off the couch at the front door. I slammed my shoulder into the front gate to make sure it was fully closed, and I turned the key in the lock. The bolt rammed home with a loud snap, signaling it was fully closed and locked.

The second it was locked, I tore the key from the lock and turned, leaping over the coffee table in a mad dash for the hallway. I bounced off the wall and used the momentum to propel me down the corridor toward the back door. It was already closed and locked when I slammed into it, but the large key was still in the lock. I madly snatched at it, and it popped free just as one of the Nosferatu made it to the ground and launched itself at the door.

It hit the cage with a loud clang, but the door held. The creature clung to the cage by its hands and feet, shaking the bars in fury. It tried to poke its rat-like face through the gap and snap its teeth at me, but there wasn't much space or give to allow the monster to squeeze through. Nosferatu are nearly bone thin, skeletal, and pale white. Despite their frail appearance, they're still strong enough to tear a human being apart.

More of them were climbing spider-like down the columns and supports as though gravity didn't apply to them. Soon, they swarmed the cage, snapping and shrieking, sticking their long, thin arms through where they could. Their skinny fingers were tipped with long, wicked-looking nails, grasping desperately. Their glowing eyes and sneering faces surrounded us as they searched for a way in.

I made my way back into the living room to find Larah tending to a few nasty-looking wounds Alex had gotten. Unlike the protection of the bubble, Alex had only been safe from the falling glass. Once they hit the floor, the impact sent shrapnel flying in all directions. While she had done her best to cover herself, the backs of her hands and forearms were a network of small cuts studded with slivers of glass. Larah had set about plucking them out with a set of tweezers that had come from the first aid kit I kept under the kitchen counter. None of the wounds looked bad, but there was a lot of bleeding.

Gillette stood vanguard over the scene with staff in one hand and his little wand in the other. At the first sign of a breach, I knew he would light the whole place up. It would be a terrifying sight, and I had no doubt he could put up a hell of a fight. But against these numbers and handicapped by trying to protect the ladies, even a wizard like him would fall.

The Nosferatu were no joke. Just a few months prior, one had nearly taken Alex's head off and killed her partner. Through his sacrifice and sheer luck, we'd made it through, but that had been with only one of the bastards. This was an entire army. At least a hundred of the things had invaded the factory. While there were a lot of them climbing the cage, there were still more in the rafters, clinging to the walls and stalking the floor, just waiting for the feeding frenzy.

We were trapped.

I grabbed my .45, for all the good it would do. It wasn't going to do much, but it was better than nothing. There were more and better tools and weapons in my armory, but at the moment, there wasn't really time to go rummaging around in there. I'm not the most organized person in the world. My system was that I know where I put stuff, but to everyone else, it looks like a mess. Even if we were armed, it wouldn't do much more than delay the slaughter, making the monsters work for their meal.

"So, what are we looking at here?" Gillette shot over his shoulder.

"Army of Nosferatu. They are fast, strong, and mean as hell," I called back, my eyes and gun scanning the cage, looking for any signs of weakness. "Same weaknesses as regular vampires. Behead 'em, burn 'em, stick 'em in the sun."

"Why are there so many of them?" Larah called out as she finished bandaging one of Alex's arms.

"No clue," I replied. "I've never seen this many altogether like this. They usually hunt alone or in small packs of three or four."

"Then we are definitely dealing with a summoner. This is likely his work," Gillette added. "He couldn't risk sending Rambo the Steroid Reindeer after us. Too valuable. So, he sends an army of these assholes to take us out. They are not as strong, but in these numbers, we would be screwed."

"Not as strong?! Are you insane?" I cried. "Just one of them is strong enough to...oh shit!" I noticed the vampire at the front cage door had wrapped its jaws around the locking mechanism and was attempting to crush it in its jaws. I ran over, leveled the gun just inches from its face, and let it have it right between its glowing red eyes.

It howled in pain as its head snapped back, and it tumbled off the door. It didn't stay down long. Shaking off the gunshot, it bared its fangs and hissed at me, but it kept its distance and didn't try the door again.

"Better check the back door. Make sure they aren't trying that same thing to get in," Gillette said, doing his best to keep an eye on all of them at once.

As I inspected the lock, I noticed something. While scored with fang marks, it was clear they weren't strong enough to bite through the steel. That wasn't what concerned me. What concerned me was the part of the frame where door locked was severely warped. In this condition, we wouldn't be able to open it. I ran into the back to check my theory and found the same thing. We had underestimated them.

"They aren't trying to get in." I said gravely, catching on to what was happening.

"What do you mean?" Alex asked, a bit of panic creeping into her voice.

"They're trying to keep us from getting out," I answered.

This was met with grave looks from everyone else as the gravity of our situation hit home. We were trapped, surrounded by the enemy, and the only people I could think of to help were trapped in here with me.

This was bad. Really bad.

Chapter 15

After about an hour, some of Nosferatu still clung to the cage, rattling the bars and snarling at us, but the rest milled about the factory, circling the cage like sharks. The factory itself was a sea of vampires. They were everywhere, covering every square inch of the place. Some perched in the rafters as others crawled over the walls like roaches. Their pale skin seemed to glow in the moonlight with an eerie pearl-like sheen.

We all sat on the floor in the kitchen. Hidden behind the counter was the safest place we could find that would still afford us a lookout while giving us some cover. Once over the initial shock, we tried to come up with battle plans, but so far, the best we had was sitting and waiting for daylight. Before the sun came up, the Nosferatu would have to flee, or else the factory skylights would let in the sun just as they had been let in. It would flood the building, turning any vampire stupid enough to stick around into ash.

"So, what do you think?" Larah asked, looking at Gillette.

"I think our summoner is making their move tonight, and the little army of freaks out there are meant to keep us out of the way until it happens." He'd been chain-smoking like a chimney the whole time we'd been hiding in the kitchen, and snuffed his cigarette before immediately lighting up another one.

"But we don't even know where they are," I said grumpily. My ass was starting to fall asleep from sitting on the floor. I peeked around the counter to make sure the vampires were still out there.

"Yeah, but they don't know that." A plume of smoke poured from Gillette's nostrils, making him look like an irritated dragon. "As far as they are concerned, we know everything, so they are playing it safe. No gloating or telling us their master plan. No elaborate, slow-moving death trap to escape from. Just covering their bases and running out the clock."

I sighed and looked around the counter again. This was boring once you got past the shock of seeing an army storm your home. I don't know how soldiers in WWI stood all the waiting and sitting around. Yeah, battles and gunfights are terrifying as hell, but the waiting is somehow worse. In a fight, it's all adrenaline and reaction, but when you're just sitting and waiting, there was just too much time to think. Too much time in your own head, just driving yourself up the wall with panic. No wonder Gillette was smoking up a storm. He was probably banking on cancer killing him before the waiting did.

"You know, this is all your fault, Halson," Alex whispered as she leaned against my shoulder. She was exhausted, having not slept last night. Then, dealing with a whole day of cop work, compounded by the shock of the sudden attack, the sudden adrenaline rush, and blood loss had zapped the last of her strength, I couldn't blame her. It was impressive she still had her eyes open. "You just had to go and jinx us."

I put my arm around her, pulling her closer. This really sucked. I wanted to apologize to her for everything. The werewolf thing, us complicating it by somehow dragging her into a deeper plot, and then getting us attacked by the very creatures that had already shaken the foundations of her life and sanity. Then there was the whole Larah thing from last night hanging over my head that I didn't even know how to go about addressing.

In the dim glow cast by the light over the stove, I could see the little white scar that cut through her lip on the left side of her mouth. It was a Nosferatu that had busted her mouth wide open just a few months ago. She had been lucky that had been the extent of her physical injuries. The psychological scars had been much worse. Not only had her encounter been a rude awakening to the real truth of the world, but it had also been a harsh reality check to how hopelessly weak she was compared to the nightmares that lived in the dark. She had reacted poorly at first, acting out in ways which both of us nearly ended up regretting.

The road to her recovery had been long and all too familiar to me. So, I had let her get her head on straight by being there as an understanding friend. But was that all there was to our relationship? Friends? Or were we something more than I'd assumed? Then there was the whole Larah thing. Jesus, what a mess social lives were. I prefer the monsters sometimes. At least those I understand.

I sighed and laid my head on hers. My own strength was starting to flag. The human body can only maintain full alert status for so long before it starts sapping your energy, and the past few days had not been easy. If we made it through this, there was still gonna be a whole other complicated issue to deal with, as Alex and I would have to sit down and talk this all out at some point. But then again, maybe I would get lucky, and something would finally manage to kill me.

If my life had any running theme, it would be that every time I hit rock bottom, life would throw me a shovel and tell me to start digging. There was no situation where being me doesn't just make things worse. And this was no exception. Because that's when things went from hopelessly bad to life having a cruel laugh.

The door that acts as the main entrance to the outside is rigged with a buzzer. Back when my home had been a factory building, this served to let the people inside know that someone was outside and to let them in. I had used it much the same way, and even after giving her a key, Alex still used the buzzer to announce her arrival.

Being in an out-of-the-way industrial complex that was mostly vacant, I don't get a lot of visitors. Very few people know where I live, and even fewer know to buzz my door. This was why it took me a few seconds to realize who it was since both the people who first sprung to mind were sitting next to me.

Then, I suddenly remembered something that made my stomach lurch.

"Oh shit, oh fuck, oh shit, oh fuck," I cursed and began digging around under the counter.

"What the hell is going on?" someone behind me said.

I was too busy tearing out junk and boxes that had piled up in the cabinets. Under a stack of drive-through napkins, I found what I was looking for and pulled it out. It was a small monitor about the size of a shoe box. One end had several wires coming out of it, and the other had a black-and-white screen. On the fuzzy screen, I could make out two people standing outside the door.

On the camera, Jake and Cassie were bundled up in winter coats as they huddled under the awning to protect themselves from the falling snow. As I watched, Jake reached out and hit the buzzer again. The Nosferatu had all paused, confused when the buzzer had sounded the first time. Now, every head turned to stare in the direction of the door. All of the blood drained from my face as I realized what was going to happen next.

"Halson, what's wrong?" Alex asked. She no longer looked tired. She was fully awake with a new flood of panic kicking her system into full throttle again.

"The trainees the Order sent me are outside, and they don't know the place is full of vampires," I said in a hollow tone. My mind felt numb, as though it couldn't fully comprehend—or didn't want to—the reality of the situation.

"Christ," Larah swore. "We have to do something, or those kids will be torn apart."

"We're trapped in here. There is nothing we can do," I said solemnly. "Even if we could call out to them and tell them to run, the Nosferatu will catch them easily."

Everyone sat in stunned silence. There was nothing we could do. Even if we could get out, we would instantly be overrun and killed in seconds, and those kids would still die. Their deaths were delayed only by seconds. I wanted to puke at the realization they would die, but we would live. It wasn't fair. I should've died so many times, but in every instance, someone else had died in my place. Life was a cruel joke.

As hot tears of anger began to blur my vision, Gillette let out a sigh.

"Aw, bugger me. Might as well finish off this bloody day right." He heaved himself to his feet and picked up his staff. From inside his coat, he took the rusted bronze dagger and fitted its hollow base over the top of his staff. He now held a rather Roman-looking spear that I think was called a pilum.

"Stay here, and don't do anything stupid," he said.

"What are you gonna do?" I asked.

"Something stupid," he replied. He gathered himself up, and the air began to fill with power again. Gillette's clothing and hair billowed as if he were standing on an industrial-strength fan. As wind whipped around him, the air crackled and sparked with electricity. The air was thick with the smell you get right before a thunderstorm, like warm copper.

He strode to the twisted cage door, lifted one foot, and then kicked it clean off its hinges. The heavy steel door didn't just pop off. The force bent the door nearly in two as it exploded free of the frame and tumbled several yards across the factory floor. It sent up sparks when it hit the concrete, taking out a couple of vampires unlucky enough to be in the way.

This got the attention of the rest of the horde, and they all turned their eyes on the wizard.

He strode out to meet them like he was walking down the street rather than into a mob of monstrous killing machines. Each footstep echoed and bounced around the building, and his staff was like a cannon going off every time it struck the floor. His eyes glowed with blinding electrical light as if he had turned into a living flashlight. He opened his mouth to speak, and it boomed as though he had been speaking through a loudspeaker. It sounded like the voice of God himself.

"I am Gillette Pendragon. Fear me, all mortal creatures who crawl upon the Earth, for I am Magus Supreme. Wielder of the primal forces who bends even reality to his will. Descendant of the great Merlin himself. I am the most dangerous wizard on Earth. He who without the universe falls to chaos...and inventor of super toast!" He struck his staff once more on the ground.

A bolt of honest-to-goodness lightning tore through the skylight and struck the tip of the spear. Like light in a prism, the blade divided the bolt into several smaller ones just as the creatures converged on him. The lightning struck the closest vampires square in their chests, instantly burning huge black holes through them. Their eyes glowed with orange flames before bursting with small gouts of fire. Their skin began to smoke and turn black as they crumpled in upon themselves.

The bolts arched from one vampire to the next in a great daisy chain of magical death as they each received the same terrifying demise. In less than a minute, Gillette's spell had reduced the entire room of beasts to piles of smoldering ashes. The air was full of the foul, greasy smell of burned bodies.

The three of us stood there, mouths open in shocked silence. There really wasn't much you can say after seeing something like that. When wizards in a mood cut loose, they really cut loose, and God help the poor bastards on the receiving end.

Alex turned to me with an inquisitive look on her face. "Inventor of super toast?" she asked, cocking one eyebrow in skepticism.

"*Invader Zim* reference," I said.

"You two are just grown man-children." She snorted, shaking her head. "Which is kinda scary when you think about the power and responsibility you two idiots have."

She was right. You would think the universe would be more careful about who it charges with saving the world. Not that I ever save the world. Mostly just Philly. I mean, it's not Detroit, so I think someone might miss it if it were gone.

"Holy crap. That was amazing," Alex called as we left the cage to study Gillette's handy work.

It really was impressive. I toed a pile of ash with one boot. It crumbled, releasing a puff of what smelled like burnt hair. I wrinkled my nose. One thing you could say about magic, it was damn effective.

"And why couldn't you have done this sooner?" I asked, a bit annoyed.

"Because you have no idea how hard it is and how much it costs to move that much magic around," Gillette said as he squatted on his haunches. I noticed he was actually breathing pretty hard. I didn't know wizards could get winded, but calling down lightning and controlling it like that would take a lot of effort.

"You gonna be okay, man?" I asked.

Gillette's face was flushed and looked more lined than usual. The whole effect made him look a lot older, like a man in his sixties trying to keep up with kids in their twenties, even though he knows it's killing him.

"Yeah, mate. In a few shakes of a lamb's tail, I'll be right as rain."

His accent came out thicker and heavier than usual. Most times, it was barely noticeable unless he was trying it on some woman, so he was more than just magically drained. I don't know much about magic, but tapping into that much power must be mentally and physically exhausting. I just hoped it hadn't been all he had because having our wizard on the bench would be a significant setback if anything else decided to go wrong before too long.

I picked my way through and around the piles to the door and opened it to let the kids in. I couldn't tell if they were shaking from the cold or from what they heard going on from outside. The inside of the warehouse smelled like the back room at a sweat lodge. That was to say, awful.

Cassie and Jake turned up their noses as they came in. Both were bundled in matching parkas dusted with snow. I had no clue what they were doing out here at this hour, given they were supposed to be on their way back home. Their training, such as it was, had ended. They should've been out of my hair and someone else's problem by now. Instead, they'd nearly walked into a vampire mosh pit and been eaten.

"Wow, what happened in here?" Jake asked as they made their way around piles of ash nearly as white as the snow outside.

"Christmas party at the office gone wrong," I said snidely. "What the hell do you two think you are doing here? You have no clue how close you just came to death."

"Um..." Cassie held a large package in her arms. "We wanted to give you this, Mr. Halson, as a sort of thank you gift-slash-Christmas present." She held the package out to me apprehensively, not sure if I was going to take her head off or not.

I sighed. You can't be a Grinch this close to Christmas. That's how you end up getting haunted by three ghosts.

"Don't call me Mister. I work for a living," I growled, taking the present and leading the two of them to the cage and the others.

"Cute kids, Halson. Are they okay?" Gillette asked as he finally stood up, more or less gaining his composure.

He looked rough. His usual effortless grace and charm were gone. He looked tired, real tired. It wouldn't have surprised me if he dropped right where he stood. We were in bad shape if this was how we were starting out the night.

"Yeah, guys, these are the trainees. Trainees, these are the guys. Don't bother learning anyone's names," I added as we all congregated in my living room, which felt even more cramped with the addition of the two kids.

"Why not?" asked Jake as he picked up a piece of pizza from the coffee table and brushed grass shards off it.

I took it out of his hand and put it back in the box. "Because you won't be around long enough for it to matter. You two are leaving, and the rest of us will probably be dead by morning."

"Wow, a real vote of confidence there, Halson." Gillette leaned back, stretching his long legs and crowding everyone else. Putting on his usual air of arrogance to cover up his exhaustion.

"They are kids, and this, whatever this thing is, is getting stupid levels of dangerous. Someone just sent an army of Nosferatu to kill us."

"An army of what?" Cassie gasped as if she couldn't believe what she'd just heard. "What happened to them?" She looked around as if she expected to see them come crawling out of the shadows.

"We killed them," I stated matter-of-factly, leveling my hard gaze at them.

They both stood there awkwardly, unsure how to act around the cadre of wary battle warn cohorts. We were hardened vets, while they were fresh-faced newbies. Each one of us exuded a certain degree of danger and exhaustion. As far as they were concerned, each of us looked capable of going toe-to-toe with countless dark entities. I didn't quite like the way they looked at us in awe.

"Okay, time to clear out. We have to find and stop some pretty nasty stuff, and you kids will just be in our way. I can't be babysitting the two of you and stop a super-powered monster at the same time."

"Jesus, Halson, you're being a bit harsh. I mean, they are vampire hunters, right? They might be of some help." Alex stood with her arms covered in bandaged scratches from all the falling glass. There were even a couple on her face. She had really got it bad with the falling glass. Even with the coffee table, she'd been lucky she didn't lose an eye or something.

"They're kids. They have no experience or real training. They will be nothing but a liability. And we don't even know when or if we will or can find this guy."

"Well, I actually have a thought about that," said Gillette.

I was about to round on him when I saw what he'd been doing. His little magic crystal on a chain was out, and it was glowing purple. It stuck straight out and tugged at the chain like a leash.

"Don't get mad, but I think I found our villain."

"What's that?" Alex breathed, mesmerized by the crystal as it hung in midair, supported by nothing but its own magical pull.

"It's a modified version of a spell Halson and I used to find the Wendigo. I used some of the ash from the Nosferatu and linked it with whatever lingering traces there were that tied it back to the summoner."

"Yeah, but won't it stop working in a bit like the last spell?" I asked.

"Nah, mate. That was with blood, a more powerful channel, but it lost power as the blood dried. The channel here is weaker, but should hold out longer. As long as we have more ash to refresh it with. Now the only question is...transportation?" He grinned, pleased with himself and looking more like the Gillette I was used to.

"What about your car?"

He shook his head as I asked.

"My Porsche is a two-seater, mate."

I looked at Alex.

"Don't look at me," she replied. "I got a lift from the wizard. My car got totaled saving your asses."

"Sorry," Larah blushed, speaking up for the first time. She had just been loitering in the back, trying not to be noticeable, like the world's most unobtrusive piece of furniture.

"Great, so how are we supposed to get to wherever to stop this ritual without transportation?" I huffed.

Cassie held up a set of car keys. "We have a van."

Chapter 16

An hour later, we were all bundled up and ready to head out. Once we had a set of wheels, what followed was a very short but vicious argument over who was coming and who wasn't. In short, the kids strong-armed us into letting them drive because they were the ones who rented it and were legally registered on the licensing agreement.

I couldn't have given a shit. Gillette hadn't either. Larah abstained from voicing an opinion, and Alex begrudgingly sided with the kids after heatedly explaining to me that police commandeering vehicles wasn't a real thing, despite what the movies said and someone getting punched. It was Gillette who got punched because I was the one who punched him. Outnumbered three to two, I relented on the condition that the kids were to remain in the car and out of danger.

After that, we had a whole gearing-up montage, complete with upbeat 80's music. Okay, there wasn't actually any 80's music, but you get the idea. The kids went to pull the van into the garage. Gillette set about gathering up vampire ashes and whatever else he needed to do his little tracking spell. Larah went through my closet to find us all some new clothing. Alex's had gotten ripped up pretty bad in the attack, and if we were going out into the winter night, we needed something warm. So, she went hunting for winter clothing and heavier jackets for the three of us.

I, on the other hand, took Alex to the back to what you could laughably call my armory. It's mostly just guns and sharp, pointy things. I restocked on silver ammo and got Alex kitted out, too. Luckily, her Glock was a 9mm, so she was able to help herself to silver ammo as well. In addition, I outfitted us with a couple of old shotguns. One was an old Ithaca M37 that had been given the Vietnam treatment, which meant it had the barrel and stock cut down, so it was smaller and lighter. The other was an 1897 Winchester trench gun.

While old, they were both still in great shape, and more importantly, they had slam-fire capability. Normally, with pump shotguns, after you fire a shot, you have to rack the pump to chamber another load before you can pull the trigger to fire the next. But in old models like these, you could just hold down the trigger and run the action. When the bolt would slam home, it would automatically fire the gun. Hence slam-fire. This resulted in a faster, almost semi-automatic style of firing. Great for short-range rapid fire when you need it.

I didn't use regular semi-automatic shotguns because they don't like to reliably feed specialty ammo. Specialty ammo was what we were running. Both Alex and I wore crisscrossed bandoleers filled with my homemade shells. Each one was filled with a mixture of phosphorus and silver filings in addition to the regular buckshot. Essentially, they were Dragon's Breath rounds with silver shrapnel shot. Nasty, but great for hunting most supernatural bogeys. I came up with the idea after my run-in with Storm Rider when I was a kid.

"Be careful with these rounds. The barrels tend to get hot after just a few rounds. And if they get too hot, the magazine tube can heat up and accidentally cook off rounds in the gun," I warned Alex as she strapped an ammo belt around her waist, holding more shells, and hefted the Ithaca.

"I'm not an amateur, Halson. I'm a trained cop and know how to handle a riot gun."

She looked damn good doing it, too. She wore an old pair of my jeans, a flannel shirt over a Rolling Stones t-shirt, topped off with an old leather motorcycle jacket I never wore. I never wore it because, on me, it looked like I was trying too hard to be hip or cool. On Alex, it looked perfect, like she'd just walked out of some 90's grunge band concert...after doing two tours of 'Nam. The ammo belts and guns gave her this whole post-apocalypse vibe.

Alex was packing the Ithaca and her Glock, rather light compared to me. I was packing the Beretta in my shoulder holster, the Winchester, my dad's 1911 tucked into the back of my pants, and my new axe.

The axe was gorgeous. It had been what was in the package the trainees had gotten me. It was beautiful. It was a bearded Viking war axe with a heavy steel head etched with Norse ruins and symbols. The shaft was an S-curve, which gave it added leverage for chopping and swinging. Leather wraps had been added to the base of the head and the hilt for better gripping. Normally, I wouldn't take a weapon into the field without testing it first, but I could feel the quality from just holding it. This was a properly made weapon, and I only had to give it a few passes from my whetstone to make sure it was so sharp it could split a hair.

It even came with a handy sheath that allowed the axe to hang from my belt almost weightlessly and kept it out of the way of my legs. The kids had said they got it as a thank-you gift/Christmas present for helping with their training. I hadn't thought I did anything really warranting such a gift. All I had done was not get them killed. But it was a pretty cool axe, and I am not one to turn down something free.

Bundling into the van, it was shocking we all fit. Jake was driving with Cassie behind him, both of them wrapped in their matching parkas. They looked like the ice climbers from that old video game. Gillette sat in the passenger seat so he could navigate with his little magical GPS. Once again, he looked more like a rockstar cosplaying as Constantine and really underdressed for the weather. I sat next to Cassie, holding a gallon Ziploc bag of vampire ashes in case Gillette's spell started to fade. In the back sat Alex in all her leather and guns next to Larah, who was dressed in leather pants and a jacket I had no clue were even in my wardrobe. The two of them looked like pissed-off road warriors. Everyone was fashionable while I, in my long coat and scarf, looked like a transient.

The rental van pulled out of my parking lot and onto the street as the wind started to pick up and the snow continued to come down. The ride was long and miserable. The tracking spell worked a little better than last time. It stayed pretty steady in one direction as we headed out of the city and started north into the countryside. We only had to stop a few times so Gillette could re-up his spell.

As we got closer, things got worse. The snow really started to come down in sheets to where Jake could barely see the road, and following the crystal was nearly impossible.

We crept through the blizzard at a snail's pace until suddenly we weren't. The snow just vanished when we crossed some magical line. It was bizarre. You could look out the window and see where the snow just stopped. It was like being in the eye of the storm. All around the edge of that metaphorical line, the storm still raged and howled. But where we were inside, it was calm. Even the clouds were gone above us, and we could see the naked night sky dotted with stars. We could even see the full moon, and it was a blood moon. A bad omen.

We found ourselves just outside the gate of an old cemetery. I mean *old* old. Throughout most of the colony states, these cemeteries date back well over two or three hundred years. Ancient places are great for burying ancient things.

Piling out of the van, we found the night air cold, but there was no wind. Whatever was creating this weird vortex was seemingly keeping pretty much everything but us out. We crept over to the cemetery wall. The first three feet of it was stone, but the next four feet of it was wrought iron with stone columns every twelve or so feet. Hunkering down behind the wall, we peered into the cemetery.

I took out a pair of binoculars and searched the grounds. In the distance, I spotted a large tree. It was an old oak, and it was positively massive. The trunk alone was nearly as thick as a small house. Its branches, naked in the winter night, spread so high and wide it was like it was holding up the sky.

At the foot of the tree, I could see light and make out figures moving around. One of the figures was tall with antlers. That was clearly our cannibal buddy. It was the other figures that worried me more. They were skinny and pale in the moonlight, stalking around the base of the tree in a wide parameter. More Nosferatu, another army of the suckers. Where were they all coming from? Who was this summoner guy, and how was he calling this many creatures to his aid?

"This isn't good," I said, passing the binoculars to Alex.

"Yeah, I was not expecting this many of the buggers. I thought we'd find the summoner and Bambi, but not another army of feral vamps." Gillette sighed.

"Can't you fire them all like you did back at Halson's?" Alex asked. I could have sworn she sounded a little too eager to see another grand display of magical destruction.

"Sorry, love, no can do. That was my one big trick, and pulling that rabbit out of my hat pretty much drained the ole batteries. I can still sling some regular spells, a bit of fire and lighting, but nothing big, I'm afraid," He admitted a bit sheepishly.

I don't think Gillette liked people knowing he had limits. I think he got off on the whole "being mysterious" and "all-powerful" thing.

"Okay, so what's the plan?" asked Lara.

"How do we stop the ritual?" I asked Gillette.

He scratched his chin and thought for a moment. "Well, we have two options as I see it, and neither is good. One, we take out Bambi, which is easier said than done, especially with all the power it's got now. The only problem is that, once destroyed, it's gonna unleash a nightmare level of pent-up magical energy. Two, we take out the summoner. He can't do the ritual, and the creatures under his control are released. But that leaves us still having to deal with the Wendigo and the same issues as option one."

"So, we're screwed coming and going?" Alex said.

"Pretty much, love. So, how do you want to play this one, Halson?"

I scanned the cemetery again, looking for anything and everything I could to come up with a plan. Sadly, there wasn't much to come up with. The Nosferatu paroled the rows of headstones in a wide area around the tree in all directions. We could sneak closer, hiding behind the stones, but once one of them saw us, it could call out, alerting the others and drawing the horde down on top of us before we could ever get close. That left only one option.

"Full frontal assault," I said, returning to the group.

They all looked at me like I was insane, and I held up my hands in warding.

"I know, I know, but it's the best option we got. Hear me out." I picked up a stick and started drawing in the snow. "Larah goes in front, using her super werewolf power to bull-doze straight through the enemy lines. You hit them, and you keep going. You don't stop for anything and head straight for the, um..."

"Altar," Gillette interjected.

"Altar, thank you," I continued. "Alex and I will follow behind you and cover your flanks. Anything coming from the sides, we can clear off with our firepower." I turned to Alex. "We aren't trying to kill anything, just keep them off her. So, you shoot, and you keep moving, got it?"

She nodded.

"Okay, and Gillette." I turned to him. He snapped me a salute. "You take the rear. Keep anything from coming up behind us and biting us in the ass. Once we get deep enough, they are going to close in around us and pin us in, so I need you on crowd control."

"Too right, Guv'nor."

"What do we do?" asked Cassie and Jake.

"You two stay in the car," I said, trying to give them my best hard-nosed, no-nonsense glare.

"But..."

"No buts, you guys are the cavalry, do you understand?" Both looked dejected but perked up a bit when they heard me say cavalry. "If something happens to us, you two have to run and tell the Order what happened. If we survive, we are all probably gonna be in bad shape and need you two to get us either home or to a hospital. Do you understand?" I asked, and they nodded.

I shepherded them back to the van. Once they were inside, I took out my dad's old .45 and checked to see it was loaded and that the safety was on.

I then handed it through the driver's window to Jake. "Just in case," I said, and he nodded.

I returned to the others, and we took a moment to compose ourselves. This was it. This was the final calm before the storm, and we were about to run headfirst into danger. When we were finally ready, we opened the gate and headed in.

Chapter 17

I nside the cemetery, all was quiet. It was that unnatural sort of silence where you can't even hear background noise that should be there. The kind of silence that means dangerous predators are around. The kind that makes the hairs on the back of your neck stand up.

Larah started stripping off her clothing, which was a smart thing. If we survived, she would want something to wear on the long ride back. Hulking out of her clothing would look cool, but we weren't here to impress anyone. She shifted forms and was unlike what I'd seen before with the werewolf the Wendigo had killed. Her shapeshifting was beautiful, almost erotic. Her form bulked as her muscles expanded and stretched her skin. Her features remained feminine as they wore off and changed, becoming more lupine.

"Wow, no wonder you two meatheads got distracted," Alex said to me when Larah's massive werewolf ta-tas sprang up and bounced in the moonlight. "She could feed a family of twelve with those."

I leaned closer to her. "Listen, Alex, if this thing goes side-ways, and it will, and it looks like things are not going in our favor...expect Gillette to bail on us."

"Why do you suddenly not trust him?" she whispered.

"Oh, I trust him. I trust him to be Gillette, and Gillette is many things, one of them is a coward. He'll even tell you that himself. Just bear in mind, he will put saving his own ass ahead of helping others."

"You have messed up friends, Halson," she replied, giving Gillette the side eye as he stared at Larah's finishing transfor-mation.

"Yeah, well, you should do the same. At the first sign we are losing, you need to run and don't look back. Focus on getting yourself clear."

Alex didn't argue. She just gave me a nod of understanding.

We now stood there with a titanic werewolf. On all fours, she was the size of a small SUV. The four of us stood as a motley crew of misfits, trying to procrastinate the inevitable. The freshly fallen snow muffled our footsteps as we made our way closer and closer to the center. The super werewolf slunk along on its belly as low as it could get, which, in the dark, made it look like a small hillock was moving through the cemetery. Its bulk gave us enough cover to hide behind as we followed.

We were able to get close enough to see the ritual site. Near the base of the tree, there was one of those small mausoleums, the kind meant for only one or two coffins. It was only about waist high, but long and low, more like a giant stone table than a crypt. Someone had put candles all around it, and the hulk-ing Wendigo stood sentinel at the head of the mausoleum. He must've been eating well since our encounter, as it was much bigger, at least thirteen feet tall, and a lot more imposing.

The beast's height only served to make the person next to it look smaller. You couldn't see their face because they wore a heavy, long dark robe with a deep cowl, but you could hear a low murmuring chanting over the still night air as they waved their hands.

The ritual was starting, and we had to do it now or never.

Larah or Mai-coh, whichever one of them was in control of the wolf form, started to pick up speed. We went from crouch-walking to a full-out sprint in seconds as we followed the charging werewolf.

Two guarding Nosferatu turned to see what was making the racket just as the werewolf lowered its head and charged right into them. They were sent flying like an old cartoon and screeching like sirens as they vanished into the darkness. That was it, the alarm was raised, and every single head snapped in our direction. Hundreds of glowing red eyes turned on us and let out matching bat-like screams. They came at us like a wave of insects, skittering across the ground with spider-like movements.

The superwolf hit their front line like a bowling ball crashing into pins, and just kept going. She plowed through creatures and headstones alike. The vampires were hurled aside, and the gravestones shattered under the impact. This shocked and surprised the Nosferatu enough that Alex and I could slip past their stunned masses with Gillette hot on our heels.

This didn't last long. They closed in on our sides in a pincer maneuver, trying to hit us from the sides where we were weakest. Unfortunately for them, that meant charging face-first into flames and flying shrapnel as we unloaded with our shotguns. One launched itself over a tombstone at Alex, and on reflex, she shot it in the face. Its head engulfed in a fireball, the monster tumbled backward over the stone it had leaped, screaming the whole way.

Another came at me, but I let it have a pair of shells right in the chest, knocking it out of the air and into one of its fellows.

The Dragon's Breath rounds did a good job of keeping them off us as we moved. The air was thick with the smell of gunfire and burning flesh. I didn't stop to look, but behind us, I saw the flashes of light and felt the heat and electrical charge as Gillette threw handfuls of fire and lighting.

Our plan was working...too well. We bulldozed our way through their lines to the ritual site. We really hadn't made a plan for this part. I hadn't really expected us to get this far. I'd underestimated just how powerful the Naaldlooshii spirit was. She had become an unstoppable freight train, able to plow through anything in our path with single-minded ferocity.

When we hit the center, there was only one thing between her and the summoner—the Wendigo.

The two giants clashed like forces of nature. The Wendigo was bigger, but the Uber Werewolf had momentum. An unstoppable force meeting an immovable object. She bounded into the big brute like an overexcited dog whose owner had just come home. But instead of slobbering kisses, she went for its throat with fangs the size of carving knives. It let out a bellow as she bowled it over and buried it underneath her bulk. It was like watching a hurricane wrestle an earthquake.

Alex and I didn't miss a step. We circled the two clashing titans, firing our shotguns to clear out the few straggling Nosferatu, and made our way toward the summoner. At a distance, the robes had made them look tall and menacing, but up close, they were a couple of inches shorter than Alex and me. Still, they held a wicked-looking dagger in one hand they slashed viciously at the air.

We leveled our shotgun at them and pulled the trigger. Instead of a reporting blast, we received a double click. Both of us were empty and would have to reload. The summoner took the opportunity to lunge at us, swinging the bloody knife. Alex simply ducked and slammed the butt of the Ithaca into their stomach. As they doubled over in pain, I socked them in the face with the butt of my Winchester.

Stumbling back, the hood fell, exposing their face. A face I recognized. It took me a few seconds to place it, but then it clicked. It was that nerdy-looking CSI tech from the crime scene. He wasn't wearing his glasses, and there was blood running down his face from where I had laid his scalp open with the shotgun, but it was clearly him.

I was about to say something when Alex jerked me backward and nearly off my feet as the two monsters rolled between us and the summoner. I had nearly been crushed by their fight. I pulled my Beretta from its holster and aimed a shot across the two bodies at him. The shot missed, going over his shoulder and causing him to flinch.

Alex came up from reloading her short gun, but as she drew a bead on him, he vanished.

It was weird to see. Letting out a hiss, he seemed to melt into his robes, becoming one with his shadow that slithered away into the darkness. And just like that, he was gone, and Alex's shot took a chunk out of the tree where he had been standing.

The chanting hadn't stopped. I didn't know if the spell was on autopilot or the summoner was just out of sight, but now we were trapped. Behind us was the ancient tree and the battling monsters. In front of us was an army of bloodthirsty Nosferatu. Gillette was doing his best to keep them back, shooting gouts of fire with one hand to keep the line at bay while firing off bolts of lightning with the other any time one of them got too froggy and tried to leap at him.

Even with the two of us pouring shotgun fire to his left and right, we were slowly losing ground. Their numbers were too great. Without Larah's wolf form to back us up, we could only slow them down.

Behind us, the Wendigo finally got the upper hand. It managed to roll over and get the top mount on the Skin-walker. It raised its boulder-like fists and brought them down over and over on the wolf's head and shoulders in a very ape-smash kind of thing. Every impact could be felt through the ground as it pummeled its opponent. There was a sickening crunching sound, and the werewolf went limp. Now, just a big shaggy rug beneath it. The Wendigo hit the downed beast a few more times to make sure before lumbering off her and toward us.

I thought we were screwed. There was no escape with the swarm of vampires encircling us. But then the area was suddenly flooded with blinding light, and the air was cut with the sound of an electric horn. Seconds later, the rental van came screaming out of the darkness, scattering vampires as it ran some of them down. It bounced and rocked, careening out of control before slamming head-on into the Bambi like it was any other deer on the road.

The weight of the van drove it back into the tree and pinned it as the doors popped open and the trainees tumbled out.

"What the hell do you think you are doing?" I yelled, equal parts fear and disappointed anger.

"Y-you guys needed help," Cassie stammered as she got to her feet, still dazed from the crash.

Jake was already on his feet, my 1911 in his hand, as he snapped a few shots off at a Nosferatu that was getting too close. The .45 did little more than annoy it, but Alex stepped in and shot a fireball into its face from her shotgun.

"You idiots were supposed to go for help, not charge in here," I snarled and pumped a few rounds into the vampire throng that was threatening to overtake us.

"But we took out the big nasty guy," Jake added.

"Took out? You just pissed it off!"

And at that very moment, the Wendigo seized the fenders of the van pinning it to the tree with its dark clawed hands, and slowly lifted it off, tossing it aside as if nothing had hurt it. Lumbering forward, it reached out and snatched up Cassie like a doll. It lifted the girl with both hands and, with a single vicious twist, it tore her in half like a wet paper towel. Blood, guts, and gore rained down from her mangled body as the monster tossed her aside like trash.

Jake let out a distraught roar of pain, anger, and sadness. He raised the handgun and fired it empty at the creature. He wasn't using silver ammo, and I had given him the .45 as more of a last-ditch emergency situation thing to make him feel better, not to go head-to-head with monsters. With one of its big three-fingered hands, it wrapped it around Jake's head and crushed it like a watermelon in a hydraulic press.

I stood there, completely paralyzed. I had done it again. I had gotten two more people killed by allowing them to blindly stumble into my life and world. They were just kids. They had no real training, no real experience. No reason to be out here fighting the fight against overwhelming odds and creatures that devoured people for fun. They were kids, for Christ's sake. They should've been going out with friends, watching movies, and worrying about classes and grades. Not riding to the rescue of my dumbass against all odds. But they had. I couldn't decide if that was more brave or stupid, but they didn't deserve this. They had so much potential and promise, and this was what they got. A horrific death in the middle of nowhere, fighting monsters that are leagues beyond their skill level.

No, not again. *Never again.* Rage surged up in me, blinding me to anything else but the asshole who had killed the trainees, *my* trainees, and I was going to make it suffer.

The Beretta was in my hands and roaring before I could even think. The Wendigo lifted its arms to protect its face as the little 9mm peppered it. Its tree trunk-like forearms erupted in little volcanoes of blue flames where the bullets struck. Bambi must've been eating his Wheaties because this didn't seem to bother him as much as it had last time. Last time, a single bullet had been enough to give him pause. Now, he just waded through an entire magazine, and it was clearly not enough.

I didn't care. I was too angry to think straight. I pulled the Viking axe from my belt. Fitting that I would use their present to avenge their deaths. Laughing like a maniac, I slashed and chopped at its arms. It was like trying to cut concrete with a dull butter knife. After a couple of swings, it got bored and swatted me away like an annoying gnat. I went over on my ass in the wet snow, the thing towering over me.

The Wendigo was winding up a punch that would smear me across the ground like strawberry jam when Alex came out of nowhere, unloading her little cut-down Ithaca into it. When the shotgun clicked empty, she dropped it, drew her Glock, and emptied the mag of silver ammo into the thing's side. That got its attention, and it swatted her, too, sending her sprawling as it turned to finish her off.

Fresh rage flooded into my body. No, not her, too. I would not let the monsters take any more people from me, no matter what. I scrambled to my feet, seized the axe, and raised it over my head. Squaring every single muscle in my scarred back, I heaved the axe with all my strength at the Wendigo. The axe tumbled end over end from my throw, but it managed to find its mark. I must've tapped into that panic strength people get in times of extreme stress as the axe head buried itself up to the eye in the beast's chest.

There was a blast of nasty, flat, greasy light, and the creature let out a pained bellow. It stumbled, landing against the mausoleum.

I charged forward as I slapped a fresh mag into my gun. Using the mausoleum as a stepping stone, I launched myself on top of the Wendigo. With one hand, I held on to its antlers. They were slimy and slick with some sort of substance I couldn't identify, like pond scum. My other hand shoved the barrel of the beretta into the cavernous eye socket of its skull face.

"When you reach Hell, tell them Bambi's mom sent you," I growled and emptied the gun into the glowing red depths of its eye socket.

Blue fire shot out of the eye hole with every pull of the trigger and report of the gun. It screamed and howled in agony as it fell back over the table-like stone mausoleum.

The slide on the gun locked back when the mag was empty, and I tossed it aside. Straddling the Wendigo, I wasn't done. It was still alive, but not for long. I grabbed the heft of the axe head with both hands and twisted. There was another of those flashes of light, and the creature screamed in pain. I worked the axe head back and forth until I had opened a rift in its chest wide enough I could see its cold, black, beating heart. It was shrouded in dancing blue flames. I didn't care. I plunged my hands into the opening and started jerking and tugging on its rancid heart. Slowly, inch by inch, I pulled its heart most of the way out of its chest.

I wanted it to see. I wanted it to watch as I destroyed its heart. This was vengeance for all the lives it had taken. I raised the axe in my other hand and brought it down on the thing's heart as its eyes blazed in fear.

"Halson! No, don't!" came a voice. I think it might've been Gillette's.

I didn't have time to heed the warning. The second the blade bit into the heart, there was an explosion of light, and I was hurled away into a world of light and sensation for what felt like a millennium.

When my sight slowly started to come back, I found myself lying at the foot of the mausoleum, half on and half off the stone slab. My ears rang, and all I could hear was a muffled, high-pitched ringing. Other than that, I seemed to be okay. When I looked down at my hands, I still had all my fingers.

The heart had unleashed a magical shockwave of energy when I destroyed it, and I had been at ground zero when it went off. My axe was gone. The heart was gone. What was left of Bambi was quickly decomposing into bone and sludge.

We had won?

That didn't feel right. We had been on the ropes, and I had gotten lucky with a sucker punch? A win is a win, and I'm not going to complain, but that felt too easy.

Something was wrong. The night had gone silent as if the world was holding its breath.

Then, the other shoe dropped. Cracks began to form along the trunk of the ancient oak tree. From inside came more of that flat, greasy green light. They crawled and spiderwebbed their way along, growing fatter and fatter until...the tree trunk exploded.

Shards of wood and splinters rained down on us as a massive crater opened in the tree, revealing it to be hollow. It wasn't empty, though. Something inside moved in the darkness. It started to unfold itself. At first, it looked like an old brown tent made of parchment paper wrapped around poles. Slowly, it unfolded itself into a vague, humanoid shape. Dry and more wrinkly than a raisin, it was some kind of mummy.

The mummy opened its mouth in a silent scream. And then came the sound of rushing wind. The remaining Nosferatu seemed terrified and tried to run, but it was as if against an invisible wind, one by one, whatever little moisture was left in their bodies evaporated, and they shriveled up and fell dead.

As more and more of them did, the mummy was doing the opposite. Each time a Nosferatu was drained, more or less, it became more whole. It became less dry and shriveled.

It took on more and more human features as it seemed to age backward. Its skin turned pale white and smooth like porcelain, its limbs long, lean, and supple. Its hair turned from short sprigs of dried grass into a long sheet of midnight black silk that flowed to its ankles. Its body was ripped with toned feminine muscle and high, perky breasts.

When it finished sucking the life force out of the vampires and had fully restored itself, it looked like the most beautiful woman I'd ever seen. She was a tall, lean moon goddess—an inhuman beauty and a face that was sharply angular with features that were a blend of both feminine and feline. Her eyes were large emerald cat eyes, and when she ran her tongue along her lips, you could see hints of her sharp fangs.

This creature was what had been sealed away inside the tree, and what the summoner and the Wendigo were trying to free.

I didn't know what to say or to do. She was...stunning. She radiated power and dominance from every part of her aura. Under the blood moon, she simply was the only thing that mattered in the world. Men would go to war and die for her beauty. Nations would rise, just to fall at her feet. She was an ancient and powerful force that only existed for humanity to serve.

I shook my head, trying to force out these thoughts. This was a form of vampire mind control. I had experienced similar tricks before, but nothing like this. It wasn't that it was more powerful, but it was more subtle. I had been able to fight them off before because it was very clear what was going on and some outside force had been trying to confuse me or throw me off. But this? This had snuck up on me like they were my own thoughts. This was dangerous. Whatever this thing was, it wasn't just a vampire. It was old and dangerous.

My sudden movements caught its attention, and its head snapped in my direction. It licked its lips playfully.

"Ah, a Hellsinger. Long has it been, mortal, since I have seen one of your kind." Its voice was like velvet and thunder. Low and pleasant and rumbling. "Fitting that one of your kind should herald my return to this plane of existence. As the Hellsingers did in days of old."

"Fuck, lady, I just got my bells rung, and I'm gonna need a minute before we do the witty banter thing," I said as I slowly got to my feet.

Her face twisted in confusion and displeasure. Not only had she been out of the game so long that my modern slang went over her head, but she also wasn't used to being addressed so casually, especially by lowly mortals. Guess they didn't have charmers like me back in her time.

"No bells have peeled this night, nor do I see any such banners to signify your armies," came her confused reply.

I just shook my head in disbelief.

"Banter, not banners, and it's an expression," I replied, looking around for my axe or gun or anything I could use as a weapon, the whole time making sure she got the message my ignoring her was a sign of how inconsequential I thought she was.

Remember that bit in *Ghostbusters* when Venkman says, *if someone asks you if you're a god, you say yes?* Same basic principle with these demigod types. You pretend you're on their level, and they think twice before squishing you.

"Without an army, you stormed the ritual of my release, sent my servant fleeing, and laid low a beast of such magical power it was able to break the seal keeping me imprisoned, with not but your bare hands, Hellsinger?" the vampire goddess asked, curious, but amused at the idea.

"Yep, pretty much mudhole stomped your lackeys and dog-walked Bambi's big fat ass without breaking a sweat. Well, I did get my clothes a little dirty."

"I do not like the way in which you address me, Hellsinger. It makes little sense and holds no respect for a being such as myself," she growled, trying to reestablish her top-dog position.

"Yeah, well, get used to it, 'cause I don't kiss no one's ass. And why do you keep calling me that?" I put some annoyance in my voice to really sell the bit. The key to bluffing well was to bluff so hard, you actually buy it yourself.

"Are you not of the Hellsinger clan? I can smell your blood, mortal. It shudders the depths of hatred and death that only the Heralds of the Abyss bear. Are you not one who stands before the gates of the Underworld and slays friend and foe alike in servitude to the dark sentinels of the outer plains?" Her eyes narrowed with suspicion.

"Lady, I'm just the asshole they send to kill you monsters when you forget your place." I smirked, really hamming up the whole aloof cool guy thing like I wasn't talking to a being who was infinitely more powerful than anything I'd ever heard of.

"And where would my place be, mortal?" There was a hint of danger in her tone as though daring me to insult her.

"Cowering in the darkness where you belong." I thought it would piss her off, maybe be the final straw, before she just up and tried ripping my head off to call my bluff.

Instead, she surprised me. She threw back her head and laughed. It was rich and melodious, somehow making me think of wolves baying at the moon. I could clearly see her fangs. Her top and bottom canine teeth were long and sharp, but dainty like a cat. Like her, they were all feminine grace, but with a dangerous edge.

"Oh, the bravado and arrogance of mortal men. It does so amuse me. I like that in my servants. The more defiance in the horse, the more loyalty it serves once broken. I will make you my champion, Hellsinger. As your name's sake, you will go forth and sing the praises of my name like times of old when the great tombs of the kings were new, and man still feared the night. You will make a worthy weapon."

She walked upon the air as easily as if it were stairs as she came towards me. I couldn't move. All I could do was look into those glowing green eyes with their slitted pupils.

"Halson, run! That thing is an ancient vampire goddess," came a yell from Gillette as he launched a magical strike against the creature.

The lightning bolt he threw never struck her. She gathered it in the palm of her hand and threw it back. Gillette took the bolt full in the chest, and I could see the shocked expression on his face as the life was smacked out of him.

The Goddess stepped down onto the stone of the mausoleum and stood before me in all her naked glory. She was easily a head taller than me, and it made me feel like a child standing before her. A great, dark shadow loomed up behind her, and Larah, in her werewolf form, came for the Goddess's back.

Deftly and without looking, she reached back and caught the werewolf by the throat. The big beast let out a strangled whimper as the ancient vampire crushed its throat. Slowly, its form melted back into that of the naked Native American woman. Larah's eyes bulged as she choked and weakly beat at the thing's arm. Her face turned purple as she struggled before finally going limp.

The vampire dropped her once she felt the struggling cease. That was power. This woman, for lack of a better word, just dropped Gillette and Larah with less effort than it took me to wipe my ass, and she did it with about the same level of concern.

Standing before me in the moonlight, she took my face in her hands and leaned her catlike face close to mine. "Enough interruptions. Enough of these weaker beings holding you back, Hellsinger. Show Sekhmet your true power." With that, she leaned in and sank her fangs into my neck. The pain of her biting me and the feel of her tongue on my flesh as she drank from me sent a flash of anger and disgust through my body that broke her hold on my mind.

I would *not* be a vampire's plaything. They had killed my parents. They had killed countless friends and innocent people. I was *not* the weak little nine-year-old who had watched my family die. I was *not* the stupid, weak fourteen-year-old at the mercy of a vampire rapist. I was Tobias mother fucking Halson, son of David Halson, great-grandson of Abraham Van Helsing, from a long line of legendary vampire hunters. I would not go down without a fight.

I craned my neck, feeling my flesh tear as she fed, and caught her ear in my mouth. I bit down as hard as I could, hot blood filling my mouth. I jerked my head, tearing her ear off with my teeth.

She let out a howl, pulling her face from my neck, her eyes blazing red with anger. Snarling in my face at the sight of her severed ear between my teeth, I spit it and a mouthful of her own blood into those haunting eyes of hers.

With a roar, and in a blind rage, she seized my head and drove it down into the cement slab of the mausoleum, and I felt the concrete shatter under the impact as my skull cracked.

I plunged through the stone top of the mausoleum and into the familiar dark depths of unconsciousness.

Chapter 18

I woke up a few days later in the hospital, shocked to still be alive. Gillette was sitting on the chair next to my bed. He looked more haggard and worn than I'd ever seen him. His face was deeply lined, and his hair was the color of old straw. Instead of a handsome man in his late twenties, he looked to be in his mid-sixties. He looked as beat as I felt.

When I asked him what happened, he just shook his head and said he didn't know. When I destroyed the Wendigo's heart, I completed the ritual to break the seal on her prison. Oops. The thing that came out was some ancient vampire, either was or at least claimed to be Sekhmet, the Egyptian goddess of blood and destruction and mother of all vampires. He didn't know for sure.

Everyone had survived, at least, except the kids, of course. Alex had been knocked out when the Wendigo had hit her. Luckily, nothing had paid any attention to her while she was out. Larah had been able to heal from her crushed throat with nothing more than a raspy voice. When I asked Gillette how the lightning bolt hadn't killed him, he just gave me his typical sly smile and laughed, saying he was immortal.

I never really know what is up with that guy, but he had clearly taken it hard on the chin this time and was trying to play it cool. When I asked about Sekhmet, or whatever that thing was, he just shrugged. After slamming my skull through the mausoleum, she'd just left. No clue why.

I had apparently been in really bad shape when the others had gotten to me. Alex had been scared I was going to die. I had a serious head wound, and there had been blood everywhere—a lot of it. It had been a panicked ride back to the city to get me to the hospital. The doctors didn't think I was going to make it. The entire left side of my skull had been a spiderweb of fractures on the x-ray. I had basically been in a coma since then. The medical staff had said it was unlikely I would wake up after that level of trauma.

Proved them wrong. I mean, I wasn't gonna be skydiving or running marathons any time soon, but I was alive.

When I asked Gillette what was next and where did we go from here, he told me we didn't. We were done. The Wendigo was dead, and the summoner and Sekhmet were who knows where. Case closed. He was getting out of town and maybe out of the country. He had stuck his neck out too much for one adventure and needed some R&R. Coward was just running away to save his own ass. Let him. I couldn't blame him. I was back to my usual post-adventure state. Beaten half to hell with more questions than answers, and left spinning my wheels until something else came along and tried to kill me.

Such is my life.

Alex came to visit a day later when she heard I was awake. I thought it would be nice to see her, but it wasn't. She was extremely pissed off. Apparently, Larah had taken it upon herself to tell Alex what happened between us the night she stayed at my place.

Alex hadn't taken it well, and they'd gotten into it. Larah had taken off, closed up her bar, and left town to do some soul-searching. She had felt pretty bad about what had happened and how Alex had reacted. She'd apparently said some pretty harsh things. By the time Alex had heard my side of the story, she'd already made up her mind and wasn't willing to hear me out. We got into a real row, and the hospital had to ask her to leave.

She just needs time to cool off...though, I think we're on a break.

I got out of the hospital on Christmas Day. Less that I got out and more like they couldn't stop me from leaving. I felt fine, and the doctors were baffled as to how I could be up and walking around with such extensive injuries. They had x-rayed me again and found the damage wasn't nearly as bad as they'd thought at first. It wasn't like a human could miraculously heal from such severe damage so quickly.

Returning home to my warehouse was pretty depressing. The skylights were still broken, and there was snow in my living room, kitchen, and bedroom. The place was a mess, and cleaning and boarding all this up was going to be a pain in the ass. But that would be someone else's problem.

What was kinda cool was finding the car parked in the warehouse. It was a 1968 Ford Mustang GTO 390 Fastback in olive green. It was the car from Steve McQueen's movie *Bullitt*. It was a dream car. I had loved the old Road Runner, but this was a unicorn in my garage. I sat in the car and ran my hands along its interior. I was in heaven. Flipping down the visor, I found a note from Larah.

Halson, I know I'm responsible for wrecking your old car, so here's my old one to try to make up for it. I'm sorry for whatever damage I did to your relationship with Alex. I tried to explain that it wasn't your fault, but you know her. She will come around. Just be patient with her. Mai-coh and I have to deal with some things, so I'm heading home, and won't need the car.

Merry Christmas,

Larah Palehorse.

P.S. Yes, I know it's the car from Bullitt. Try not to kill yourself.

That was kinda cool of her. I felt sorry I had upturned her life here, but I was a little happy I had made a new friend. One more person to mourn me at my funeral.

I trudged inside and sat down on my snow-covered couch. Just a few weeks ago, Alex and I had been having a quiet movie night, sitting on this same couch, eating pizza and watching some dumb action movie she liked. I would've wished that those days could've gone on forever, that things would never change. I hate change. Change is never for the better.

There was a note and my .45 lying on the coffee table. This time, from Gillette.

Sorry, I drank all your crappy beer. Check your refrigerator. Merry Christmas.

Your favorite wizard,

Gillette

I got up and stomped over to the fridge. It was mostly empty. I checked the crisper drawer at the bottom and heard a loud clink. Inside were two rows of beer bottles. It was some fancy foreign stuff, obviously German, and very expensive.

Just the kind of thing Gillette would do.

I took a beer and closed the drawer. There was a loud clink again, and I opened the drawer for a look. It was full again. Neat. I took out a few bottles and closed the drawer, and when I opened it, it was full again. Seriously neat. A bottomless, never-ending magic drawer of beer. Very cool.

I took a bottle, opened it, and sat back on the couch. I sipped the beer as I looked at the notes. It had been a rough year. I had lost several friends, two trainees, my office, my car, nearly my life several times. I'd gotten a girlfriend, I think. Lost said girlfriend, I think. Had sex for the first time. That was one in the win column.

Wow, a lot of living in the last year.

I never thought I would make it to thirty. Vampire hunting is a tough life. But it had always been so abstract. I'd never really fully actualized death as more than a concept. Even when facing monsters like Storm Rider, my uncle and the hunting party had showed up and saved my ass at the last second. I don't know. I sort of kinda believed that someone or something would show up last second and save my ass like always. Like how Gillette believed he was immortal.

Now, here I was, looking death in the face. It's different when it's not a monster breathing down your neck or some accident like a car crash. It's too quick that you don't have time to really think. You just make peace with it.

Yet, here I was, sitting on my couch drinking beer, my gun in my hand, contemplating my own suicide. There was no other way. I had been bitten by a vampire. That in and of itself wasn't bad in the long term. You will heal, deal with the trauma, and move on. But I had done something stupid. I had bitten the vampire. I had gotten her blood in my mouth and inevitably swallowed some.

Meaning, I was going to turn into one.

There was no doubt about that. It was already happening. I was healing from my injuries too fast. I felt fine. I don't mean fine, as these injuries didn't bother me. None of my injuries hurt or bothered me. I had wracked up a lot of them. I always felt a tight pull in my back and some stiffness from the scar along my spine. But today, I felt like I could do backflips and cartwheels. My joints didn't ache, and I wasn't tired.

I finished the bottle of beer and wanted another. I was starting to feel thirsty. Just a little. A sort of slight dryness in the back of my throat. Not a good sign.

I was not going to be one of those...those things. I would not become the very thing that killed my family, that I dedicated my life to hunting. I've seen what they do and what they are, and I will not allow myself to become the same.

Checking to make sure the 1911 was loaded with one in the chamber, I cocked the hammer, put the barrel in my mouth. Tasting the cold steel on my tongue, I took a deep breath and closed my eyes. Putting my thumb on the trigger, I counted, then exhaled and opened my eyes, my finger tensing on the trigger.

Confused at what I was seeing, I paused and took the gun out of my mouth.

"Wait a minute...you're supposed to be dead," I said to the man sitting across from me.

Afterword

Tobias Halson: Werewolf Hunter is the last in the bunch of works I wrote prior to 2016. That is to say, back when I was still a young unjaded writer and the world wasn't the worst possible timeline. But I digress, this sequel was actually finished before the first book. If you've read the afterword in Tobias Halson: Vampire Hunter, you know the story.

I was about 2/3 through writing it, and got the idea for this book, loved the idea, and started working on this book without finishing the first. This book ended up changing the whole course of the series. Primarily due to one character: Gillette. Gillette was fun to write. Mainly because he is an iterative designed character.

Readers of my books know that when it comes to Urban Fantasy, two of my favorite series are the Antia Blake series by Laurell K Hamilton, and the Dresden Files by Jim Butcher. Butcher I discovered back in high school first reading Fool Moon. I fell in love with the series, and while I like the character of Harry Dresden, he falls prey to the problem of most of the Urban Fantasy protagonists: a Martyr complex. Most of the reasons his life is miserable and the suffering he endures is self-inflected through this egotistical idea that he has to suffer so others don't. At least, more so in the early books.

While noble, it's an exercise in masochism. One of the ideas Jim touches on in his books is the idea of "Evil Harry," who isn't really evil. The character pops up as a manifestation of Harry's Id, which isn't really evil so much as it is a version of Harry that he is a more egotistical version. One that is a bit more self-involved and puts his own priorities above others. Butcher straight up mentions that this version is basically just Harry if he used his powers for himself more, and gave into his more baser instincts and desires.

I really liked this idea. What would Harry Dresden be like if his ego wasn't so wrapped up in playing the savior to everyone. In the current books, Dresden is more self-involved due to a number of factors driving him to reevaluate his priorities, and is being influenced by dark forces.

I wanted a Dresden that was self-centered as their default. A character was just as worn down and jaded, but that led them to playing fast and loose with everything, rather than only in the service of others. So, I ended up with a wizard character, who was the opposite of Dresden. Where like Halson, Dresden is a lot more Spartan and thread bare in their lifestyles and shut themselves off from others as a way to manage their trauma, this character would be more puckish.

Brash, charismatic, maybe a bit detached from the mortal day to day world. While a novel idea, it has been done before. John Constantine is a good example of doing this right, however a good example of doing this badly, in my opinion, would be Nate Temple from Shayne Silver's Temple Chronicles.

The Temple Chronicles, to me, are just...just bad. Among the myriad of problems I found with the books, the main character, Nate Temple, is the worst. Like Harry Dresden, he is a wizard, like Harry, he is an orphan, like Harry, he is talented...however, unlike Harry, Temple is also rich, a genius, and perfect at everything. He is basically magical Batman. Everyone knows him and everyone fears him, and because of how the character is written, there is never any stakes or real threat. He is overpowered and perfect in every way with no flaws. Temple is like an 80's action hero—they walk through a hail of bullets uninjured. If they do get injured or tortured, they take it with stoic silence, only to shrug it off seconds later. They are less of a human being and more of an unfeeling robot—the character equivalent of that kid on the playground with the "everything proof shield."

Dresden is more like Jackie Chan. While extremely capable, he barely makes it through by the skin of his teeth and is just as surprised as you are that he survived whatever dumb stunt he just pulled off.

Stakes, that is the difference between a good character and a bad character.

This was one of the major concerns I had when creating the character. The problem with magic is that, it's magic. It can do whatever you want it to do. A guideline Fantasy writers try to overcome this by creating a "magic system." A guideline of rules which magic has to follow to keep it from being overpowered and world breaking. However, this regularly causes problems and breaks down when the plot demands it.

I struggled with this, trying different rules and systems to limit Gillette's powers. Nothing worked until I hit on an idea. In addition to the novels, Butcher also writes short stories set in the Dresden world. A couple of the more interesting ones are the ones that are not about Harry. Two come to mind, one from the perspective of his brother Thomas, and the other from Karen Murphy. A common theme in both is the lamenting of not having Harry on their side. This got me to thinking about how the other characters see him.

Harry himself tells Thomas in one book, Blood Rites I think, that the only time he really sees Harry is once a year for about three days after some Big Bad has been warming up to killing him by first beating him senseless. While we see the series through Harry's eyes and know every little thing, fully aware of the stakes, and the costs and how human he is, everyone else sees him as a superhero.

Both unstoppable force and immovable object.

They only see him standing toe to toe with monsters and gods, and throwing down on what looks to be an even playing field. Leading to many characters in the newest books to question just how human he really is...

This got me thinking about another interesting character: Riddick.

Before Vin Diesel let his ego ruin the character, Riddick was pretty cool. What the sequel and video games failed to understand about what made the character so compelling in Pitch Black was how the character was portrayed. Not as a person, not as some generic gravely voiced badass action hero, but as this morally gray force of nature. The things he does, the way he acts, puts him in the realms of the almost supernatural. You are ever sure of what he is going to do, but when he is on screen, he is fun and fascinating.

This gave me the solution to my magic problem, or at least, let me kick the can down the road to deal with at a later date. I could just portray Gillette as this whimsical force of nature. I could allow Halson's point of view to show Gillette as this insane powerhouse, while hinting at cracks in his armor. Then, later on, I can retcon anything I need to as 'well that was just his POV.' It's literary cheating, but hey, all's fair in love and war, as they say.

What I didn't expect was how Halson and Gillette would bounce off each other. Gillette, while meant to be a fun comic relief character, was not meant to be an incompetent gag character, and I couldn't have Halson addressing every interaction with him with insults and violence. So, Tobias had to change.

He went from being a forty-something grizzled Noir Detective to a younger, more hip Marvel style anti-hero. I ended up having to discard my original plans for the character once I got attached to the duo. Of course, if you have read the first book, you know I went back and completely changed the character and the story unfolded differently.

Another weird thing happened in this book that I didn't realize until I started editing this one for publication...I totally Raiders of the Lost Ark-ed Tobias in this one.

For those who aren't terminally brain dead from years of movies and TV like I am, there is a glaring issue with the first Indiana Jones film. Aside from it being the perfect adventure film, Indiana Jones has zero agency or effect in the film or its outcome. If you removed him from the film, it would still turn out exactly the same. The Nazis would still find the Ark, they would still open it and get their faces melted, it just would have happened sooner.

This one issue drives fan nerds crazy. It doesn't change how good the film is, it's just weird once you see it. And you can't unsee it.

I kinda did the same thing by accident. In the first book, it's more of an 80s action film, with that film primarily being Die Hard, with a dash of Lethal Weapon, if you pushed those films through the filter of Josh Whedon's Buffy the Vampire Slayer.

However, in this book, I gave Halson the Indy treatment. He had no agency or effect on the outcome of the story. In the first one, Halson is on the hunt, he is plying his trade as a vampire hunter. He roots out and kills the main villain at the end of the book. Here is his being drug along by other characters.

The Order drags him into training the Newbies. (Who, like Tobais, are references to another book series I liked as a kid: The Animorphs). Alex drags him into her murder case. Gillette drags him along to hunt the Wendigo after they find the blood. Halson doesn't instigate anything. He is purely reactionary, and if in-

stead of answering his phone at the beginning of the book he just went in and kicked up his feet, the gang probably would have had a relatively quiet Christmas, and Sekhmet would still have ended up getting freed.

I honestly can't tell if this is just bad writing or genius on my part.

As for the, um, sex bits, I don't generally write about sex. It's tantalizing, but not necessary for my work, and as stated above, I am a bit fan of Antia Blake. It's a great series. If you have not read it, go check it out. The first three books are amazing. Don't get me wrong, the rest of the series is good, too, to a point, but the first three are the gold standard. The issue I have with the series is the same issue that all of her fans have. From about book 11-20, Hamilton gets lost in the sauce, and these books lose the thread of the plot. Somewhere around book 20 or 21, the series returned to being almost purely Monster Hunting.

I did not want to fall into that pitfall, but to be honest, I kinda wrote myself into a corner with that whole virginity thing. It also gave me a way to drive a wedge between Tobias and Alex. Things were moving too fast, and I didn't think I would be able to pussy foot around the whole will-they-won't-they thing for more than a couple of books without either committing or blowing it up. So, I blew it up early. You're not here for smut. You're here for Monster Hunting.

Okay, let's address the ending.

Yeah, bit of a dick move to end on a cliffhanger, but that was written back in 2014-2015, and yes, I did plan on a third book. And while it's been roughly ten years, I still only have the rough idea outline, if you will, though I don't outline, of the story. I have had other things on my plate, and my priorities were more focused on my horror writing. I tried to write a standalone Gillette novel, but that didn't work. I started a spin off series in the Halson universe featuring a character that was supposed to appear in the third book, but that stalled out. That begs the question...will there be a third book?

Well, it does already have a title, *Tobias Halson: Vampire*, and the framework of what was a planned follow up novel *Tobias Halson: Monster Hunter*, and there was a planned prequel/sort of novel featuring Halson's grandfather in WWI/WWII fighting Nazi vampires. Beyond that, there isn't much that isn't more than notes on a legal pad. I don't really plot or outline when I write. I prefer organic freeform writing, but I do take notes. As a writer, it's always good to write down ideas and such on a scratch pad or Word document so that you don't forget it. I have different word pads, documents, and folders for all this stuff. I am just not very well organized.

Who knows, if the series does well and readers like it, maybe my publisher will ask for the third book. As long as I am alive, I guess there is always potential for the series. I currently have about three(?) projects already in the pipe and about five to six more WIPs hulking on my desk wanting my attention.

But one thing at a time, Dear Reader, and this is where we must part ways. Until next time.

CHECK OUT THESE OTHER GREAT READS FROM ROWAN PROSE

John Evans is the author of the pulse-pumping book "Midnight Falls." He also writes the "Tobias Halson Hunter" series and various short stories. Inspired by greats like Stephen King and Gary Brandner, he loves all things "old school" horror, and often claims his purpose is to give readers a little bit of fun Lovecraftian escapism from the scarier real world.

www.ingramcontent.com/pod-product-compliance
Lightning Source LLC
Chambersburg PA
CBHW020801310726
48969CB00002B/643